HOPE AND DESIRE

SASKIA WOODHILL

A catalogue record of this book is available from the National Library of New Zealand

Lightpool Publishing

www.lightpoolpublishing.com

PROLOGUE

If someone had asked Abigail to name the most unlikely things to happen, finding a naked man on her doorstep on a freezing winter night would not even have been on her list.

Long after the event she would think back to that evening and wonder at herself.

Why did she not dial the emergency services instead of doing the simple things she thought would suffice when he fainted and feel in the door?

Why did she not feel alarmed when he asked, "Why are you in my house?" before he fainted?

Instead she simply wrapped him in a warm rug and waited for him to wake up.

But then, if she had done what most people would have done, the entire story would have had a different outcome instead of changing her life the way it did.

When the doorbell rang at fourteen minutes past one in the morning, Abigail knew before she opened the door that something had happened to Mike. Somewhere in the back of her mind there had always been a dark shadow of apprehension. She rarely thought consciously of the dangers he faced as a police officer, but a little hint of threat had been with her on a subconscious level ever since she met him.

She unlocked the door and the look on the superintendent's face made it clear without a word being spoken - Mike was dead. He opened his mouth, but before he had time to say anything Abigail swallowed and swung the door wider open. 'Come in Gordon' she said in a tight voice she didn't recognise as her own.

They sat in the kitchen with only the light above the stove on, facing each other across the kitchen table. 'How did it happen?' Abigail couldn't believe that her voice sounded so normal now and nearly casual. Surely she should be in floods of tears and sobbing through the words, but here she was calmly analysing her own response and deciding that she was in shock.

'He was stabbed.' Gordon's face creased in distress. 'They were doing a raid on a drug house we've been watching for some time, and this guy suddenly rushed at Mike and stabbed him. They got the ambulance there immediately, but there was nothing they could do. The knife had a long blade. The paramedics think it probably sliced into his liver, and he bled out internally. I'm sorry, Abigail. He wasn't just a valued member of the team, but he was such a good friend to us all – always ready to support anyone who was troubled. I can't get my head around it.'

'Neither can I,' said Abigail and noted that her voice was now trembling. 'I knew it could happen one day, but now that it has, it seems unreal. But wasn't he wearing his stab-proof vest?'

Gordon frowned. 'Oh yes, of course he was, but this guy had an underhand grip of the knife, so he was stabbing upwards under the edge of the vest. It happens now and again. That kind of grip has long been known to inflict terrible damage if the knife enters just below the ribs.'

When Gordon left, after Abigail had turned down his offer to ask one of her friends to come over, she went back upstairs not quite sure what she should do now. But once she was in the bedroom she instinctively went to Mike's side of the bed and lay down with her head on his pillow, pulled the quilt over herself and finally cried.

The week that followed was a mixture of busy hours with endless phone calls and funeral arrangements, interspersed with periods when she didn't know what to do with herself. Being at home during a working week and feeling unsettled meant that nothing seemed like the right thing to do. But out of the blue the perfect solution presented itself, and she started spring cleaning. Not that it was springtime, but the kind of cleaning she engaged in was very thorough and had a mindless quality that suited her mood. Every piece of furniture was moved, every skirting board dusted and every cupboard and drawer in the kitchen turned out, wiped and sorted. She emptied the drawers in the bathroom and checked the use-by date on every single product including the toothpaste and polished the inside of all the windows. The physical activity was the respite that enabled her to present a reasonably calm face in her interactions with funeral directors, family and Mike's colleagues who called with flowers.

Casseroles and cakes were left on her doorstep, and she put the contents into aluminium containers and then straight into the freezer. At the end of the week a row of dishes and bowls were lined up on the back seat of her car with a thank-you card in each one ready to be delivered back to those who had dropped them off, but she had eaten nothing other than toast, yoghurt and bananas since the night when Gordon came.

month later Abigail sat at the kitchen with her much younger sister Astrid. They hadn't been together in Abigail's house since the day of the funeral, when the house was so full of people that Abigail hardly had time to have a proper conversation with anybody.

'I still can't believe it,' said Astrid and looked as if she was about to burst into tears. 'I miss him so much. He's always been there, kind of looking after me ever since I was about nine or ten when you first met him. You know, the way he used to hug me and put his arm around my neck and pull me close, and then he'd tell me what I've done wrong or what I should be doing - and the way he did that always registered with me. If he'd been my father instead of that guy mum kicked out when I was tiny, I would have been a better person than I am now.'

'You are a perfectly lovely person,' said Abigail and reached across the table to give Astrid's hand a squeeze. 'Mike was so proud of you. He used to say you were his substitute daughter - he really loved you.'

'Not the way I don't seem to be able to handle money.' Astrid managed a crooked smile. 'He didn't like that, but then neither do I, believe it or not. But I don't seem to have a grip on that kind of thing even now. Perhaps I never will. You know how I keep telling you I know exactly what's coming out of my account and what I can afford to spend, and then four days later I realised my rent's due or the power bill or some other damn thing, and I have to call you and say help.'

'We'll work on it, darling. Don't panic – we'll continue to rehearse what it is you must do to keep track. I do wish you'd use that spreadsheet I set up for you because if you did, you'd realise what was coming up before it happened.'

'I know. I'll try.' And then a thought struck her, and she looked devastated. 'But you won't be able to afford to help me any longer when I stuff up - you only have one income now.'

'Of course, I'll help you,' said Abigail and wondered how much she should tell Astrid. Perhaps it was better to only tell her the official part of the story, because she wasn't sure yet how she felt about what Mike's lawyer had told her, and what it would mean in the future.

'Mike had life insurance through his work, so I'll be able to pay off the mortgage and invest a bit of money, and my job is pretty well paid,' she said casually. 'Mind you, that doesn't mean that you should stop trying to balance your budget, just keep on trying. It's something everybody can learn, and you're a clever girl, so there's no reason why you can't get a grip on it.'

After the funeral some changes took Abigail by surprise when they happened. Of course, she had realised without thinking about it that those of Mike's colleagues, who had offered to help with anything that needed doing on the property, would not be in constant touch, but the general shift in approach among her friends surprised her. Three months down the track she suddenly took in the fact that a transition had taken place, and now her and Mike's friends seemed to have moved on from being sympathetic. Or perhaps they hadn't moved on, but their sympathy was overlaid with a layer of normality that said as clearly as if they had spoken the words that it was time to look forward and not dwell on her loss. Though Abigail had never been in the situation of comforting a friend who was recently widowed, she found it hard to get used to the idea that talking about Mike seemed to be regarded as "dwelling on the past". Not that anyone said it, but it was as clear as daylight that people would rather she moved on.

· · ·

When Aaron, who had been Mike's partner on a lot of jobs, called a month later and asked if she wanted to go to the movies that weekend, Abigail was already busy both on Friday and Saturday nights with close friends, and Aaron said he'd ask her again. His approach surprised her because he didn't like her and made no secret of it when they met for drinks or dinner with Mike's team. At times he had been openly dismissive when she voiced an opinion or introduced a topic, as if what she said was of no interest because it came from a woman. After a rather unpleasant exchange with him over drinks a year ago, Abigail had decided to never have any kind of political discussion with him again. His already far right leanings had become more hardline over time, and he was never shy about voicing them in a social context. Some of his opinions struck her as extreme and political discussions tended to become uncomfortable, close to confrontational. Mike told her that the best way of dealing with Aaron, when he became insistent in a discussion, was to laugh at him, which made him hesitant and often calmed him down.

'I've been doing just that for a long time, and it works. He hasn't got a sense of humour, and it disconcerts him when he can't figure out why I laugh,' he said to Abigail as they drove home after one particularly trying Friday night pub session with his colleagues. 'Aaron knows he won't change my mind, and I know I can't change his, so I tell him it's pointless to even start these discussions.'

'And how does he take that?' wondered Abigail, who had always found Aaron hard to deflect, stubborn and hell-bent on winning every argument.

'He lets it go – and if he doesn't I just tell him to shut up. No way am I going to spend time at work being pestered by an extremist. One time quite recently I said if he didn't stop I'd ask for another off-sider and that hit home – he's not tried it with me since. So, either laugh at him or just tell him you're not going to debate with him next time and make it sound as if you mean it.'

Abigail didn't expect Aaron to ask her out again, but only a couple of weeks after his first invitation he did ask, this time by unexpectedly turning up on her doorstep one night when she was in the middle of eating her dinner.

'No thanks, Aaron,' said Abigail without opening the door any wider than she had to. 'I'm not ready for dating or anything like it, so if you don't mind I'll just go back to my dinner before it gets cold.'

The look he gave her was hard to define and unsettling, and she thought about it off and on during the rest of the evening and tried to make up her mind what it had meant. In the end she decided it was possibly two emotions blended into one. First a quick flash of something like dislike, and then an assessing look as if he was evaluating her in some way. It had made her feel dismissed and scrutinized at the same time. He couldn't possibly be interested in her in any real way, she thought, as she lay awake in her dark bedroom, unable to go to sleep as usual since Mike's death. She had always known that Aaron didn't like her, and it was personal, it wasn't just that she could hold her own in a debate, so why this sudden interest? And so soon after the funeral too; it seemed inappropriate from every angle.

As time went on she stopped thinking about it, and if she had considered it again she would have regarded it as a temporary aberration, something rather strange, but in the past.

$\mathcal{A}$ couple of months after Aaron's appearance on her doorstep, Mike's sister Rosemary came to stay for a week, and on her last night they had dinner at Abigail's favourite Italian restaurant with Astrid, and Mike and Rosemary's uncle and aunt. As they followed the waiter to their table Abigail noticed to her surprise that Aaron and one of her courthouse colleagues were sitting in the bar and turned her head away. Reluctant to risk any kind of approach she took care to sit with her back towards the bar, but while she studied the menu she continued to wonder. Seeing the two of them together puzzled her because in all the years she had known Aaron he had never mentioned he knew Frederick, and neither had Frederick ever commented on knowing Milke's partner. Shortly after sitting down, when she got her phone out to show Rosemary something a friend had posted about Mike on Facebook, she took the opportunity to use the dark logon screen as a mirror, saw that the staff door to the bar was now closed and heaved a sigh of relief.

Over the following months Aaron made two further approaches, both unexpected and slightly creepy. On Abigail's birthday he sent flowers with a card wishing her a happy day and expressing the hope that she would soon feel like "picking up where we left off". After reading it Abigail stood as if frozen by the kitchen bench vacantly looking at the flowers with a sense of unreality. What on earth did he mean? They had never had anything that could possibly be referred to as having ended or paused, and which could therefore be picked up where they left off. After a few minutes she snapped out of the feeling of mental dislocation, threw the card in the wastebin and said out loud, 'The man's either stupid or a fantasist, but the flowers are nice – I'll put them in the living room.'

But dismissing the strange message was not as easy as throwing away the card, and the vague unease it had generated stayed with her for a couple of weeks. Then a month later, when the cold autumn weather was just setting in, there was a parcel in her letterbox containing a luxurious pale blue merino shawl and a card from Aaron saying he was thinking of her these cold days and hoped to see her soon.

Now a tinge of alarm crept into her mind and

the word "stalker" appeared for the first time. Does this qualify as stalking? she asked herself and left the shawl lying on the wrapping paper, unwilling to even touch it. Two or three approaches, flowers and now a present. He had never been further inside their house than the front hall before the day of Mike's funeral, and he was never involved in their social life apart from work functions, plus the fact that he didn't like her – so what else could it be? And for the hundredth time she realised how losing Mike had changed her life, how much she missed the feeling that someone always had her back, that whatever happened she had someone to discuss things with, and not least, the comfort of knowing there was one person in the world who always worried about her safety. Irreplaceable, she thought now and felt her eyes fill with tears.

The full extent of Mike's protective instinct had not been revealed until after his death when Rob Alderton, Mike's lawyer, contacted Abigail and asked her to come and see him. She would never forget how she had sat in the chair across from his desk and simply stared at him, unable to say a single word. After a few moments of silence, while Rob waited for her to respond and she remined silent, he said, 'I would like to tell you exactly what he said when I asked why he was spending so much money on a private life insurance policy when the police already had his life adequately insured,'

'What *did* he say?' asked Abigail, still hardly able to believe what she had just been told. Rob smiled and shook his head. 'Probably the most surprising thing Mike ever told me, and over the years he told me quite a few surprising things. He said that if anything happened to him, he wanted you to have a fantastic surprise and be able to do whatever you wanted for the rest of your life. He was a very unusual man.'

'I know,' said Abigail sadly. 'There might not be another man like him in this world – he was one of a kind.'

'He didn't want you to know in advance. He said we'd keep it as a nice surprise, so if he met with a fatal accident you would find out as you have now – with no inkling of what he had planned for you. He got the police department to pay part of his monthly salary into our trust account and we paid the premium, so you wouldn't notice - for the last six years. I've just cleared things with the insurance company, provided proof of death et cetera and now the money is here for you to invest. You need to decide what you want us to do now. Invest some and put some in a high interest earning account in the bank or buy another property, perhaps. Just over four and a half million is a large amount and far too much to just sit around doing nothing in the way of earning interest or dividends.'

But now, standing there staring at the blue shawl, Abigail felt convinced her gradual suspicion that Aaron had found out about the insurance money must be right. Rob would have left work, but she wanted to talk to him right away, so she called his cell phone and hoped he wouldn't mind when he heard what she had to tell him.

'Hi Rob,' she said a moment later. 'I'm sorry to call you after office hours – I hope you're not just about to sit down to dinner?'

'I'm still at work. I had a backlog of correspondence, but I've just dictated the last letter. What can I do for you?'

'It's a bit of story, but first I want to ask how it worked with the payout of Mike's life insurance, the private one. Did that money become part of the estate? I mean, was that part of the total when the probate was applied for?'

'Oh no, it was never part of Mike's estate. You were the beneficiary of the policy, and the money went straight to you. Nothing to do with the probate. But why are you asking? Is something wrong?'

'I know my colleagues could have found out about the estate via the probate process, but I'm wondering if a couple of guys have also heard about the private insurance policy.'

Rob was getting concerned, and Abigail knew him well enough to pick up on his change of tone. 'What's happened for you to ask about this? Are you having some kind of problem at work?'

Trying to sound casual and not too concerned Abigail said, 'I think it's a bit like stalking, though I'm not sure that's the right word, but it does concern me. It's an ex-colleague of Mike's who's taking a sudden interest in me, very unexpected and quite determined.'

'What's he doing? Tell me exactly why you've become alarmed about this. And don't try to tell me you're not alarmed – I can tell it's upsetting you, so I need the details.'

Twenty minutes later Abigail ended the call with a feeling of relief at Rob's advice. In the morning she would take the scarf, in its original wrapping and with the card inside, to the police station and say it was for Aaron.

'There's no need to include a message,' Rob had said. 'Don't ask to see him or thank him in any way, no explanations. Leave it at reception and just say it's for Aaron. And take a photo of the open parcel and his note before you do it and of the writing on the outside of the parcel. I think documenting every move this guy makes would be wise. The more reasons we get to warn him off the better.'

Her second task would be to contact the alarm monitoring company and get some changes implemented as a safeguard. 'It's not that he's likely to harm you, is it?' Rob said reasonably. 'But if he gets to be a nuisance, and if you can prove he hangs around outside or keeps coming to the house uninvited, then you can get a restraining order as a last resort. And before that a letter from me saying you prefer to be left alone might do the trick.'

When she told Rob about her vague feeling that Frederick was somehow involved in Aaron's plans, whatever they were, he hesitated. 'There was nothing in the estate Aaron wouldn't already have known about, I don't think. Mike's will was just the usual things, his car and his share of your jointly owned house, his pension fund et cetera. All the frontline cops are insured to the same extent, and Aaron would have known that already, so even if he got your colleague to check it out, there would have been no surprises. It's a bit vague, the whole thing.'

Not knowing how Rob would react to what he might see as a slur on his team Abigail said slowly, 'I'd hardly think the police insurance payout would be enough to tempt Aaron. I've always known he doesn't fancy me, he doesn't even like me, and he ignores me if I have an opinion and talks over me. He's very right-wing, and I really don't know how Mike put up with him for so long. But the possibility of getting to share the private insurance payout might be tempting enough for him to put up with me. I wondered if he knows someone who works at your firm – someone who might have told him?'

She held her breath waiting for Rob's reaction, but he seemed unfazed. 'It's possible, of course, people do gossip. But quite aside from what motivates him, there's something else I want you to do. Document all his moves up to now and send me a list with all the detail you can think of – and then get your security system upgraded as I said, so you have all the bells and whistles, and continue to keep me informed.'

Later that evening she wondered if she should talk to Mike's boss Gordon about Aaron's behaviour but decided that discretion was the key for now. There was no need to make this semi-official, not yet anyway. In the morning, she would talk to the security company about her alarm system and see what they could suggest in the way of an upgrade.

4

Since Mike died Abigail had got into the habit of declining invitations that seemed like potential dates rather than just a friendly drink, or occasions when well-meaning friends would try to pair her off with someone single or recently divorced, which had happened a couple of times. Aaron had now called her a few times, as if he realised she wouldn't let him in if he turned up uninvited on her doorstep again, but she had turned down his suggestions about going for a walk or a drink. Her problem was how to make him stop pursuing her, seeing that turning him down repeatedly didn't work. There had also been a couple of propositions from men she and Mike had known well, men who seemed to presume that a woman, who was used to having someone in her bed and now found herself alone, would welcome advances from men she had never indicated she found even remotely attractive.

'Not to mention,' said Abigail indignantly to Rosemary on the phone one night with a glass of wine in her hand, 'that both those guys are married! Shameless doesn't even cover it, does it?'

'Quite common, I think.' Rosemary sounded more amused than surprised. 'I've heard about it before after divorces and separations – I suppose some men see it as an opportunity worth trying, don't you think? And perhaps they take for granted the woman they approach won't tell their wife – if they think that far and engage their brains instead of their willies.'

One evening when she was upstairs cleaning her teeth after dinner her phone pinged with an alert and the updated security app showed her a car like Aaron's parked on the far side of the road. She could see the outline of the driver's face turned towards the house. Standing there with the phone in her hand and the toothbrush still in her mouth, she continued watching, mesmerised by the idea that she was watching Aaron watching her house, and he had no idea, then after a few minutes he drove away. Over time she collected several instances of Aaron outside her house, learned how to save clips of the camera footage and created a folder called "Stalker" on her hard drive. It was hard to imagine why he would spy on her and the only thing she could think of was that he was determined to find out if she was going out with someone else.

After a while she developed the habit of checking the peephole in the door before opening it at any time of the day or night. Not that she thought Aaron was likely to become dangerous, because why would he? He wasn't trying to harm her, he was trying to charm her, unlikely as that seemed. But he might try a more physical approach, and the idea of struggling with him made her shudder with distaste. She told herself she was being alarmist and there was no reason to think he would go to those lengths, but the thought remained like a little shadow in the back of her mind.

When Frederick stopped beside her late one afternoon, when she was tidying her desk before leaving, she didn't react at first to the way he looked at her, and it was only after she turned down his invitation to go out for a drink or dinner that she realised what that look was. It was speculation, very like the look Aaron had given her when he turned up on her doorstep. And her mind snapped back to the memory of seeing those two having a drink together the night she went out for dinner with the family. Surely they couldn't be working in tandem; how would that even work? But later the idea of Aaron and Frederick colluding would return, and she wondered if Aaron had recruited Fred to have a go, seeing he himself had failed. But it seemed outlandish and more like a film script than real life, so she told herself to stop being ridiculous and pushed the thought aside.

Am I a commodity now? she wondered. A relatively young, relatively attractive widow with considerable assets. And how could Frederick possibly imagine she would say yes? They had worked together for several years, but there had never been an iota of attraction between them. His motives had to be opportunistic, either hoping for casual sex or access to her money. After studying his face for a long moment while these thoughts flew through her mind, she said calmly, 'No, I'm not dating, but thank you,' and turned aside to pick up the bag.

As she walked away towards the reception area she could feel him still standing beside her desk looking after her, and she sensed that Jane behind her glass partition had been watching their exchange. She didn't turn her head to look directly at Jane knowing how likely she would be to call out something supposedly teasing and probably inappropriate, or even inflammable.

Crossing the car park, she pulled her collar up and buttoned her jacket. Dusk was falling and a swirling wind swept dry leaves into the corners and against the wheels of the cars. As always she pressed the central looking button before she even started the engine. This was a habit that started after an incident when a woman had been stopped on the road close to their house in an attempt to steal her car, and Mike had insisted that she always locked herself in.

'You never know,' he would say. 'This is supposedly just another street on the edge of town, but it's also a minor arterial rout to the Badlands. And these days you could be stopped anywhere by a fake accident or something, so just do it please.'

She knew he was right, and she sometimes saw people trying to thumb a lift, presumably heading for that outlying suburb that Mike always called the Badlands, as did all his fellow police officers. Not that she would ever pick up a hitchhiker, but as Mike had said, if the car was always locked, then if someone stepped out into the middle of the road and forced her to stop, she was safe.

5

Tonight, she headed first to the library because Friday was their late night when they didn't close until seven and she thought she might be able to persuade Astrid to come along to the gym. The contrast between the warm interior of the car and the outside when she got out of the car surprised her. Even on that short drive the temperature had dropped noticeably; it was going to be a very cold night. Inside the library the bright lights and the low hum of the air conditioning created an atmosphere of quiet calm. It's like a capsule of warmth and silence, thought Abigail as she looked around for her sister, such a restful place to work. A moment later she spotted Astrid walking across the gap at the end of an aisle pushing a trolley loaded with books. Abigail came up behind her sister as she stood with a book in her hand staring at the shelf in front of her.

'Are you reciting a portion of the alphabet?'

Abigail laughed when Astrid jumped. 'Last time I came in and found you shelving books I actually heard you whispering a sequence of the alphabet. Remember when you were little, and we used to do it at the breakfast table.'

'Oh hi! Are you sneaking up on me from behind now, so you can catch me out? Yes of course I'm reciting the alphabet. Just like I recite part of the eight times table if I need to work out what six times eight is. Just as you taught me when I was in primary school - and it's still the only way I can figure out the right answer. But we all take turns replacing returned books, and I'm way slower than the rest of them. They look at each other and grin and say "bye – see you later" when it's my turn to push the trolley around. They know they won't see me for hours.'

'I'm on my way to the gym,' said Abigail. 'When do you finish? Do you want to come? I'll wait for you if you like.'

'No thanks. I've had enough exercise this week. I helped Biffo move, and he had dozens of cartons full of books and CDs, I think my arms are four inches longer than they were last weekend.'

'What do you mean, you helped Biffo move? Have he moved in with you?'

'Oh God, no - I'd never have him as a flatmate, he'd be impossible. He's so untidy and he stays up half the night playing video games or watching sport. He'd ruin my life.'

'Oh, good,' said Abigail. 'Not that I don't like

him, and I know you've been friends since middle school, but I can just imagine what an irritating flatmate he'd be. If you're having trouble finding someone for your spare room I can ask at the office. We've got a couple of new girls, and they might know somebody.'

Astrid pulled her phone out of her pocket to check the time. 'Just about time to pack up and go home. It's not my turn to cover the last two hours this week.'

She manoeuvred the trolley around the corner of the shelf and said over her shoulder, 'I'm not worried about the spare room being empty. Now that I've gone from probationary pay to the real pay level I don't really need anybody to share the flat. And thank you for the hundredth time for finding me a nice flat with such low rent. I'll get someone eventually, but I'm not in a hurry. I'd rather make sure the person I pick is the kind of person I can live with.'

Abigail said goodbye without further comment and thought how lucky it was that she had been able to intervene when Astrid had to move and couldn't find anything convenient within her price range, apart from a small flat with access up steep stairs from an alleyway. And it was pure chance that it happened the way it did. She was in the supermarket and bumped into a woman her mother worked with many years ago, and during a short conversation she had mentioned that Astrid was having a hard time finding a flat in the central city at a price she could afford, and even as she spoke she realised what she should do and hatched a plan.

'I want to help her, but I don't want her to know,' she said to Barbara, who now ran a successful real estate company of her own. 'Sometimes she finds it hard to balance her budget. So if you find a nice rental, say a modern flat with two bedrooms, we could perhaps set it up, so I pay part of the rent, and Astrid doesn't know that the remainder she pays isn't the full rent. Do you think that could work?'

Only a couple of weeks later Barbara called her and said she had found the perfect flat, and she had spoken to the landlord about the rental arrangement, and he promised not to mention it to anyone else.

Outside tiny snowflakes swirled in the wind and Abigail's black car had a thin coating of snow on the roof. It was early for snow, and it was getting colder by the minute. As she drove away she wondered, not for the first time, if she should simply buy a flat for Astrid. She could do it, but she worried it might make Astrid's life too easy with the result that she would never learn to control her spending.

Ever since Astrid was a toddler Abigail had looked out for her and picked her up and dusted her off when things went wrong. She had babysat her, taught her to count and generally acted as a spare mother, which was sorely needed with a real mother who was an ambitious real estate agent, hardly ever at home and always involved with a new man. And now, she thought wryly, our mother lives on the Gold Coast with yet another man and she's no damn use to either of us.

After some thought Abigail decided she couldn't be bothered with the gym on a Friday night after a hard week and drove home. She clicked the remote attached to the sun visor at exactly the right distance from the house to be able to drive into the garage without stopping. As always she heard Mike's voice in her head: 'I think you should stay in the locked car until the door has folded right down. It doesn't waste more than ten or twenty seconds, but it means you're totally safe.'

Sometimes she would tease him and say, 'You know what? I think I'll stop all that fuss with the garage door and staying in the car until the door is down - it's such a drag when I'm dying to get inside to pee.' He always said the same thing, 'Please don't, you're important to me and I've seen enough tragedies in my job.' And she would reach up to kiss him and tell him she was only joking.

After her talk with Rob and the subsequent

upgrade of the security system a new end-of-the-week habit had developed, and now she booted up her laptop and flicked through the footage captured in the last few days. The new, so-called intelligent software allowed her to change the outline of the sensor zone outside where movement triggered the camera to start recording. She tended to leave the red outline of the zone where it was, at what seemed a reasonable boundary. It went at wide angle to the sides and across the road to take in the sidewalk on the other side, as recommended by the security consultant she had talked to when she explained she thought she had a stalker.

'Just ignore the rules,' he said. 'Or the unwritten rules – we don't have specific by-laws like some cities, but it could be regarded as invading people's privacy. Just forget all that! You want to be able to see if this creep parks on the far side of the road and watches the house, not just if he's on this side.'

With the sensor zone set to cover the width of the road every car that passed, every delivery truck and pedestrian started the camera recording, and at first the sheer number of short clips nearly overwhelmed her. Then a couple of weeks after the upgrade the security man called and said to download the new version of the software, which allowed a user to prime it to identify specific objects.

'Perfect!' she said when he explained it. 'I know exactly what he's driving.'

Since she uploaded images of Aaron's SUV the

security app had alerted her several times when his car was parked on the far side of the street, usually at night, but he hadn't approached the house. Tonight, she had been alerted when he drove slowly into the sensor zone just after she parked outside the library, and she had watched him stop opposite her house and stare across the road. She saved that little recording along with the others in the Stalker folder to forward to Rob. Sometimes she wondered if he sometimes parked further away and approached on foot. Would he walk around to the back of her house, try to see if she had someone there? Tonight, for no particular reason she clicked on the app settings and set the camera to record continuously.

Abigail was well aware that some would see her precautions as an obsession, and maybe it was, but after her talk with Rob she had spent some time online researching stalking. What she found was alarming, multiple sources quotes instances of "passive staking" that had only been discovered after a sexual attack or an assault took place, mostly on women. The BBC website had a podcast about murder victims whose killers had quietly stalked them over long periods of time but not been regarded as a threat of violence when reported to the authorities – until it was too late. She didn't think Aaron was any kind of physical threat, because what he was surely after was a relationship that would allow him to persuade her to pay for whatever luxury he wanted, or perhaps marriage for even easier access to her wealth.

She closed the laptop and went to make herself a meal, while in the back of her mind she wondered when he would next approach her directly. For some reason she couldn't quite work out, he had made no further attempt to talk to her since she returned the shawl, but maybe he was working up to it, sitting in his car outside and studying her movements. Perhaps he hoped to catch her just as she came home and get out of his car to approach her, because he wouldn't know that she always drove straight into the garage. But it was hard to second-guess someone whose nature was so different from her own, and now she dismissed her thoughts and sat down with vegetable lasagna from the deli with her Kindle for company and told herself she must stop thinking of Aaron and his strange tactics.

Curled up in the corner of the sofa after dinner she started re-watching the first season of Killing Eve on Netflix. Jane had talked about it in the lunchroom the other day and said how much she enjoyed it the second time around, far more than she had expected to.

'Far more depth than I remembered, more back story,' she said, gesticulating with her sandwich that threatened to disintegrate. 'Kind of like I'm discovering a layer of seriousness I never noticed the first time round. And it came back to me how much I love Sandra Oh's quirky eyebrow – it was like meeting an old friend again.'

'You're older now,' commented the glamourous new administration assistant, who invariably seemed to have a sensible, down to earth comment at odds with her selfie-queen appearance. 'And probably wiser, so you're noticing things that went right over your head the first time.'

Now Abigail discovered she too enjoyed the drama at least as much as the first time she saw it and the evening surprisingly turned into a binge-watching night. Since Mike died she had not spent a single evening binge-watching, but why she couldn't quite put her finger on. Maybe it had to do with how they used to look at each other, and she would say mock-seriously, 'It's getting late, perhaps we should go to bed? You're on the early shift tomorrow.' And Mike would pretend to hesitate before he said, 'Maybe just one more.' They were both night owls and often one more turned into two more or even three, and they didn't get to bed until way after midnight, early shift or not.

Abigail had just checked the time and decided not to start another episode when a sound made her sit up straight to listen. Faint but distinctive, the sound of someone turning the handle on the front door. Alarmed she got up, muted the TV and walked slowly towards the door. She stopped with a feeling of disbelief as the door handle turned again. Very slowly she walked forward and put her eye to the peephole and nearly exclaimed out loud: a completely naked stranger stood shivering with cold on the top step. Behind him the snow still fell softly into the cone of light from the outside lantern. The pinched look on his face and how pale he was, concerned her, the last thing she wanted was to find a dead body on her doorstep in the morning. Slowly she turned the lock knob and pulled the door open with the security chain still in place. The man outside stared at her through the narrow gap and said in a disbelieving voice, 'Who are *you*? What are you doing in my house?'

'I live here, this is my house," said Abigail, but before he could reply his knees buckled and he grabbed the door jamb to support himself. Quickly she unhooked the chain and opened the door wider just as he tilted forwards. She reached out and tried to catch him, but he was heavy and limp, and she had to let him slide to the floor in a semi-controlled way. He lay half in and half out of the door with snowflakes on his dark hair like tiny stars, and his skin so cold and pale it looked luminous. She must get him inside and out of the cold! Grabbing him by his upper arms she tried to pull him inside, but it was slow work with many adjustments of grip and angle before she had him fully inside and could close the door.

What now? wondered Abigail and closed the door, panting with exertion. Maybe I should call an ambulance, wonder what's wrong with him, or maybe it is only that he is so chilled? She knelt beside him and put her hand on his cheek which was cold and damp. She moved her fingers to the side of his neck. His pulse was steady but seemed slow, and she wondered if being so cold had caused his heart to slow down. She knew very little about hypothermia but looking it up now would take too long and the first priority must be to warm him up. Rapid ideas streamed through her mind with lightning speed, things to be considered later - why had he been outside in this weather without any clothes and with no shoes? Had he been robbed? Maybe she should call the police rather than an ambulance. Or maybe both?

Speculating about who he was and why he was in this state could wait. She ran to get the fleece rug from the back of the sofa and covered him, tucking it in around him until the only part visible was his head, considered only for a moment, discarded the idea of an ambulance, and ran upstairs to get a pillow from the guest room. She knelt beside him and gently lifted his head so she could slide the pillow under his head then tucked the rug securely around his shoulders again. Putting her face close to his she said, "Hey, can you hear me?' but there was no response, not even the flicker of an eyelid.

Back in the living room she turned off the TV and muted the lights before returning once again to the hall and after a few moments' thought she made up her mind. He didn't seem to be injured, his pulse was steady, if slow, and he looked as if was asleep rather than unconscious, exhausted and cold but hopefully not in danger of dying. The question now was how he would react when he woke up. Would he become aggressive? She couldn't risk going to bed with her uninvited visitor lying on the hall floor, likely to suddenly wake up and maybe panic. He was obviously confused, but why? What if he was mentally ill or had a head injury?

Once again she knelt beside him and ran her fingers gently through his thick hair to feel if he had a lump or a cut on his head but found nothing to indicate an injury. With the small armchair from the living room pulled into the doorway and the thermostat turned up a couple of degrees, she sat down and took a deep breath. From here she could keep an eye on him, and if she fell asleep she would wake up the moment he made a noise or tried to get up.

Then another thought popped into her head – clothes! She raced upstairs and opened the long wardrobe that ran along the sloping roof in the guest room. It was only recently she had finally packed Mike's clothes away, but she hadn't yet got around to get rid of them. She knew the only sensible thing was to take them to one of the charity shops, but she had put it off more than once. At the time of packing things into the boxes she had written on each one what was in it, not knowing if the second-hand shops would take everything, and now those little scribbled notes were useful. She pulled out one box after another until she found the one with "thermals, jeans, fleece" written on the side, and then the one labelled "jackets" and started lifting things out and stacking them on the floor beside her. The stranger was probably much the same height as Mike, she thought, quite a bit leaner, but these would do.

She carried a bundle of clothes downstairs and put them on the chair beside the little table in the front hall. Her unexpected visitor lay in exactly the position he had been in since she tucked him in, but his face was a shade less white, which made her feel comfortable about her decision to not call the emergency services. Once again she checked the pulse on the side of his neck and decided it was steady enough not to worry about.

With most of the lights in the house turned off Abigail settled into the chair with the book she had started reading on her Kindle the day before, but her brain didn't take in a single word. Her mind was full of questions and concentrating on the words was beyond her. Instead, she tried to imagine where he could have come from, why he was naked, and most of all, why he had said with such conviction that this was his house.

7

*J*ust before five o'clock in the morning the man on the floor stirred and groaned. Abigail surfaced abruptly from semi sleep with a crick in her neck and saw him trying to get up, but his legs were tangled in the blanket. She jumped to her feet and knelt beside him, pulled the rug off his legs and put a hand on his shoulder to stop him struggling.

'Wait,' she said. 'Take it slowly. You might get dizzy if you stand up too fast.'

'What happened?' His deep voice was hoarse and confused. 'Did I fall? Who are you? Why are you in my house?'

'You fainted, and you were very cold, so I covered you up. Let's save the talking for a bit and get you dressed.'

He looked down at himself. 'What?! Why am I naked?'

It nearly made her laugh. This was what she too

wanted to know. 'I have no idea. I opened the door and there you were, stark naked and freezing. And then you kind of fell in the door, or half of you did, so I dragged you in and wrapped you up. You've been asleep for about five hours.'

He shook his head and ran one hand through his hair, his expression confused and worried in equal parts. 'I don't understand what happened. Have you got something I can put on? Maybe a dressing gown?'

'I put some clothes for you there,' she said and pointed at the chair. 'They were my husband's, and I hadn't taken them to the second hand shop yet. I think they'll fit you pretty well, perhaps a bit big. I'll find a belt for the jeans shortly, but now I'll go and make a hot drink while you get dressed.'

She left him sitting on the floor, turned the kitchen wall sconces on and pulled the blind down over the side window. Heaven knows what will come of this, she thought, but having nosy Mrs Paxton, who always got up very early, see her with a strange man in her kitchen at five in the morning was too much to contemplate. It would be gossiped about with the neighbours in no time at all, and until she knew who this seemingly harmless stranger was, she wasn't prepared to let anybody know he was in her house.

He joined her in the kitchen just as the kettle had boiled and she was busy making two mugs of hot chocolate. Glancing at him she could see he was just about to ask her yet again why she was in his house, so she pre-empted him.

'I'm not sure what you mean when you say this is your house.' She tried to sound calm and casual, as if this kind of conversation with a stranger, who had until five minutes ago slept naked on her hall floor, was normal. 'I live in this house, and I've lived here for several years. I think you must have mistaken this house for your own.'

His gaze swept around the kitchen, and she could see doubt creeping in. 'Isn't this 37 Loring Road?'

She nodded. 'That's right, but it's still my house – and please sit down. Where did you come from? I can't believe you were outside without any clothes in this weather, and there's no car outside. Did you walk?'

He sat silently looking down at the table for so long she thought he had lost track of the conversation, then he looked up, exhausted but clear-eyed and focused. 'Something's terribly wrong. I don't know what it is, but there's something very strange going on. Can I please have something warm to drink? Warm water will do.'

'I've just made you a drink of hot chocolate. I thought it might be a comfort after what you've been through - whatever that was.' She handed him the mug and put a plate of biscuits on the table before she sat down opposite him. His colour was better now, but he looked very troubled, confused and frightened.

'Where did you come from?' asked Abigail. 'And what's your name?'

'My name's Harry. I've just returned from a job in South America and ...' His voice tapered off, and he looked into the middle distance for a moment. 'Something happened at the airport.' He stopped again and shook his head, and he looked down at his left arm. 'That mark on my arm - did you see it?'

Abigail nodded. 'It's terrible scar. Is it from a burn?'

'No, I think it's to do with that weird thing that happened at the airport. I didn't have it before.'

Slowly he pulled up the sleeve of the fleece sweatshirt, and they both looked at the wide mark from his elbow nearly to his wrist, dark brown and shiny.

'What happened at the airport? And please drink your chocolate while it is hot, you probably need something warm inside you.'

He didn't reply and seemed deep in thought, so after a moment Abigail reverted to the question of why he thought this was his house. 'Are you sure you live at 37 Loring Road?'

'Oh, for God's sake, of course I know where I live! I bought this house when I moved back here from Hamilton, six or seven years ago.'

Once again he looked around hond she could see how he studied the details, took in the objects on the kitchen bench, the blinds pulled down over the windows and the potted herbs on the windowsill. When he spoke again his voice was slow and dreamlike. 'This isn't what our kitchen looks like. But it *is* the right place, I can tell you every room and every cupboard in this house. I can describe the whole layout and *prove* that I know this house. I know where the electric circuit breakers are and how the door to the linen cupboard in the upstairs hall opens the wrong way, which is a nuisance. I don't know what's going on. Did I have a stroke?'

Abigail tried to think of something she could suggest, something that would not only enable them to work out what had gone wrong with his memory, but which would also reassure him. Maybe he had forgotten that he had moved again, wiped out short term memory, maybe a shock of some kind had caused this.

'Do you know what day it is?' She was thinking of things she had read about the kind of things you should ask someone who might have a head injury.

'It's Friday, no wait - that was yesterday - it's Saturday now.' He pulled the sleeve down and ran one hand up and down his scarred lower arm, thought for a moment. 'It is, isn't it?'

'That's right' said Abigail. 'It's just after five on Saturday morning.' She reached for a biscuit and her hand nudged the phone she had put on the table. He sat up straighter and stared wide-eyed at her phone where the black lock screen now showed the date. '2026? Why does your phone say 2026?'

She stared at him and thought she must have missed something. He was definitely confused, possibly concussed. Getting the day right, and then not knowing what year it was seemed like a very worrying thing. If anything, she would have thought he'd get the year right and the day wrong. 'It's definitely 2026,' she said gently. 'There's no doubt about that. What did you think it was? The year, I mean.'

He's forgotten a year or two, she thought and watched his agonised face. He's been in some kind of accident and lost some of his memory and now he's terrified because he can't understand what's happened.

She could see desperation in his eyes. 'It's 2029,' he said and moved his head slowly from side to side, as if he couldn't believe that this conversation was taking place. 'I flew to Brazil in 2029, and I seem to have returned in 2026 to a house that was mine and is now yours.'

They stared at each other, both silently trying to come up with an explanation and failing. She could see how convinced he was, there was no doubt in his mind, and Abigail decided to change the subject. Dwelling on the confused subject of which year it was would get them no further, so for now perhaps a completely different topic would provide some relief.

'I don't think I told you my name,' she said. 'I'm Abigail. Why did you go to South America?' A safe topic, something unthreatening to talk about for a few minutes. Maybe he would feel less uncertain, and she would gain some useful information.

'I was there on a job. I'm a geologist and I

sometimes supervise explorations in other countries, mostly to do with finds of rare or valuable metals. This time it was titanium.'

'How long were you there?'

'Just over two weeks, most of it at a remote site way inland, staying in some prefabs they had airlifted in. I always enjoy site work, it's a nice change from sitting in my office writing reports and analysing data.'

'You were very cold when you fell in the door,' said Abigail, encouraged by how readily and clearly he described the site in Brazil and what he had been there for. 'I really worried about how slow your heartbeat was because you were so chilled, but I thought if I wrapped you up warm you'd be all right. I did check your pulse a couple of times, and I could feel your skin warming up.'

'Thank you,' he said politely and drank some of his hot chocolate. 'This is helping too. I haven't had hot chocolate since I was a child.'

His forehead creased and he closed his eyes and sat absolutely still while Abigail silently studied him and wondered what he was thinking. After a few moments he opened his eyes, cleared his throat and looked seriously at her. 'This is incredible. It simply can't have happened – but it has. Can I look at your phone please? I've never seen one like that.'

She pushed the phone across the table and watched him pick it up and look at it intently. 'So, it doesn't fold?'

'No, I don't like those. I want to be able to see

the time without having to unfold it. But surely you've seen a phone like this before. It's just a common brand of smartphone. What's yours?'

He looked around as if he was expecting to see his phone somewhere in the kitchen. 'Mine is a Flexus 9,' he said. 'Did I drop it outside?'

She shook her head. 'I don't know. You had no clothes on and no shoes. I didn't see a bag when I open the door. I only had a quick look outside, but I couldn't see anything. I was too worried about the state you were in to investigate properly.'

She got up and pulled the blind aside a little but there was nothing to be seen. 'I have no idea where your possessions have disappeared to.'

And then she had an idea that might shed some light on this strange situation. 'Wait here,' she said. 'I'll get my laptop, and we'll check the security camera footage. We could look at it on the phone, but if we're going to look at it together it's easier on a bigger screen.'

'Come and sit on this side,' she said when she returned with her laptop. 'Sit beside me so we can both see the screen at the same time.'

She couldn't define why she suddenly trusted him and felt no fear or apprehension about what he might say or do. There was no real reason to feel so relaxed, and she knew without thinking about it that it had nothing to do with pity. Something he had said, or perhaps the way he said it, had unlocked total trust. It was the first time since she met Mike many years ago that she had experienced this sensation with a man.

She clicked on the security system icon and selected a time to start watching, about half an hour before she had opened the front door.

'I'll just scroll through this. I've set it to record continuously at the moment because I've had a little bit of trouble with an unwanted visitor, who turns up uninvited at inconvenient moments, and sometimes I prefer to pretend I'm not home.'

The scene they saw was her front garden and a portion of the street outside. The wind had dropped since she got home, and light snow was falling. The wheel marks she had made when she drove up the short driveway to the garage still showed. Apart from that there were no marks in the smooth cover of snow. No footprints on the path to the front steps, no footprints across the lawn from the garage driveway to the front door. She fast forwarded past the occasional car going past and kept her eyes on the rapidly changing images on the screen while she talked.

'I went into the house through the connecting door from the garage and ...' she said and then, before she had time to continue, on the screen right in front of their eyes, Harry materialised in the snow halfway between the garage driveway and the front steps. One second he wasn't there and then he was, lying curled up and stark naked in the snow. Quickly she paused the recording. 'My God! How did that happen?'

They looked at each other, both speechless, then Abigail rewound the recording and started it again, going very slowly this time. And once again, from looking at a pristine sheet of snow with not a mark on it, suddenly out of nowhere a naked man was lying on her front lawn, coiled into a foetal position. He didn't fall to the ground, he was simply there, where there had been nothing a second earlier. She continued slowly forward, and they watched him until a couple of minutes later he stirred and slowly sat up.

'Look!' exclaimed Harry. 'You can see that mark on my arm.'

Abigail let the recording slowly move forward and they watched Harry get to his feet and look around. He turned in a full circle, and they could clearly see his expression now that the outside light on the garage had been activated by his movements. He looked stunned and confused.

'I remember this – I was looking for my things,' he said. 'I couldn't figure out what had happened. I thought I must have been in some kind of accident. I don't think I realised that I was naked, I just knew I was cold.'

As they watched he moved slowly across the snow covered lawn towards the front steps leaving footprints behind him. Abigail stopped the recording, got up and went to the front hall, opened the door and looked out. The snow had stopped falling, and though it must have continued for some time after Harry appeared out of nowhere, she could still see the patch where he had lain. A roughly oval patch in the snow and his footprints, slightly less crisp now that some snow had covered them, but still visible. And no marks anywhere else apart from the vague remnant of wheel tracks on the garage driveway. She closed the door. returned to the kitchen and met Harry's questioning eyes.

'I don't know how that happened, but as you said - it did. If you look outside the evidence is still there, it's as clear as day. You simply materialised in the middle of my front lawn and then you walked towards the front door leaving footprints, but that's all. There's nothing more.' She thought for a moment. 'I'm going to save this part of the recording as a separate file because I think it's important that we keep this. It's evidence that it really happened the way we say, and we might need it sometime in the future.'

His eyes were fixed on her face; the implication of what she had just said was as clear to him as it was to her. They were in this together and had to protect him by their joint efforts, though from what threats she couldn't imagine. A man, who had mysteriously arrived out of thin air, a man who seemed to have come from some other time or dimension; there was no manual for this situation. Her only thought was that they must be very careful and consider the consequences of everything they did from this moment on. Imagine the headlines, she thought, the speculation, accusations of fraud and deceit. It would be devastating, not only for Harry but for herself.

Harry got up and went into the hall, and she heard the door open then shut after a few moments. 'I think I'm right,' he said on a note of disbelief when he returned. 'That mark on my arm must have something to do with what happened at the airport – and how I got here. I didn't tell you before, I got sidetracked, but it kind of explains several things in a mad kind of way.'

His face was very tense now and his body stance betrayed how deeply disturbed he was. Some normality might be good for both of them before he started on his explanation in case it was a traumatic story, and it was nearly breakfast time now. She made a quick decision to create a diversion to make him calmer.

'How about we re-start the day in a more normal way?' She tried to sound causal and relaxed. 'It's nearly breakfast time now and we both need a shower, and then you can tell me about the airport incident and take your time over it. And something more might come to mind if you think about whatever happened while you get tidied up. There's no hurry, is there?'

He hesitated for only a second. 'OK - thank you! A shower would be great, and if you don't mind I'll see if I can find something else to wear in those boxes you mentioned. I'm feeling slightly overheated in this sweatshirt now.'

'Oh God, I forgot! I turned the central heating

up last night when I found you. I thought if the whole environment was warmer you might recover quicker, but I'll turn it down to normal now - but you don't need to wear fleece inside. There are several more boxes in the cupboard under the eaves, literally everything Mike had apart from his underpants and worn out socks, which I threw out. You might even find some shoes that fit you.'

8

Upstairs Abigail got a clean towel out of the linen cupboard, noted that it would indeed be better if the door open in the other direction and nodded to herself. 'Take as long as you like in the shower. You can look through all the boxes later and decide what you want to put in the chest of drawers. I think you'll find most of it useful. What size shoes do you take?'

'Forty-three most of the time.'

'I think that's the same as Mike's, or maybe one size smaller - he had big feet. So you have your shower now and we'll meet downstairs when you're ready.'

'You go first,' he said politely.

'I'll have a shower in the bathroom next to my bedroom, don't worry about me!'

'Is there another bathroom now?'

That simple question confirmed once again that everything he had told her was true, which included that he had come from 2029, the strangest thing of all. This stranger, who knew there had only been one bathroom, and who was so surprisingly calm despite his apprehension, who had proved in numerous ways that he had lived in this house, was telling the truth. Coupled with what they had seen on the security recording it was total proof, and not a shred of doubt remained in her mind. Somehow this man had come from some unknown future or dimension of time, and he compared the house to how it had been in his future, if such a thing was possible. She nearly laughed at the oxymoron of recalling something that hadn't happened yet, but she had to accept it.

'We added another bathroom a couple of years after we bought the house,' she said. 'We couldn't have children, but our relatives like to come south for the skiing and waiting for your turn in the bathroom was inconvenient when everyone came back from a long day on the slopes.'

He smiled with a glint of sly mischief. 'So you converted the bedroom beside the master bedroom? Did you make a doorway beside the wardrobe and make the wardrobe bigger? Katrina and I kind of mapped out how it could be done.'

She stared at him, still stunned by this additional unarguable proof that he knew this house as if it were his own. It's crazy, she thought, but there is no other explanation.

'That's exactly what we did. Half of that

bedroom became a new bathroom and the other half a large walk-in wardrobe.'

They looked silently at each other and there was no need for words. He had once again proved a point, an unbelievable point when looked at through the lens of normal life but a fact all the same.

Standing in the shower Abigail mentally sorted through the few facts she had and tried to decide how to proceed. She couldn't possibly take him to hospital. There was no need to make him more traumatised than he was already, and she felt sure now that whatever had happened wasn't going to be solved by medical science. And it wasn't a case for the police. He was just a man lost in time who needed help. Over breakfast she would remind him to tell her about what had happened at the airport, along with a raft of other things she wanted answers to, but right now it the most important thing was to proceed slowly and let him acclimatise in a calm way. Apart from his knowledge of the upstairs lay-out the thing that was most convincing was the security recording. She had kept a careful eye on the timestamp at the bottom corner of the screen when they went through the recording the second time, and there were no seconds missing, no gap in the timeline. Not that it was necessary, she thought, because how could he have ended up curled up like a pretzel in the middle of the lawn like that, leaving no footprints? Nothing she regarded as normal could explain it.

Her inner discussion continued while she dressed, and she found herself mapping out a sequence of things to look up and check, various ways of helping them understand how this had happened,

She was in the kitchen making coffee when she heard his footsteps on the stairs, rapid and athletic. He came into the kitchen with his thick hair damp and ruffled, dressed in jeans and a grey sweatshirt with Harvard printed on the front.

'My husband didn't like that sweatshirt and hardly ever used it.' she said. 'I used to wear it sometimes, just around the house, though it's far too big, but I decided I probably wouldn't use it again, so I put it in the box.'

'Because it was his? Too much of a reminder?'

Wow, she thought. He's very surprising, that wasn't the sort of comment I expected from a man. 'Yes - because it was Mike's. It makes me feel ...'

'I get it,' he said and sat down at the table again. 'I had one nearly like this too, navy blue. Did Mike go to Harvard?'

It made her laugh. 'God no, he was a cop, detective sergeant. A very good one - I've got his police bravery award for outstanding courage upstairs. Did you go to Harvard?'

'I did my PhD there.' He looked closely at her. 'Listen,' he said, and she could tell he was deadly serious. 'Whatever caused this and however it happened, I think we should keep it to ourselves.' His eyes never left hers, as if he was determined to spot any hesitation even if she didn't voice it. 'We don't know how it happened, but I have a ghastly feeling that if we told anyone they would immediately think I've had a breakdown, that I'm deluded - and God knows what they would do to me. Haul me off to the nearest mental hospital? So, if you agree I'd be very grateful for your discretion, until we understand more about it. I can tell that you've accepted it, strange as it is, and that's great, but the rest of the world will draw other conclusions. People might suspect me of being a fraud, wanting attention in media or whatever.' He paused for a moment. 'All I need is some place to hide out – somewhere safe where no one will see me, perhaps in your garage or a shed.'

'No way! Are you crazy? You're going to live in the guest room and just stay out of sight until we know more.' Abigail nodded to herself. 'If we're going to manage to keep this quiet you'll have to stay inside until we've worked out a way of safely introducing you to the world, but you'll have a normal life – none of this hiding-in-garages stuff. Just relax!' She smiled at his serious expression. 'I feel as if I've taken a wrong turn and walked into someone else's reality. This is so weird!'

'Tell me about it! And don't forget I'm not even in my own world. I've been moved to whatever we should call this different world. It's not my past, or you wouldn't own this house.'

'Timestream,' said Abigail. 'Let's call it a timestream. It's a word from a book I read some years ago. In yours it's 2029 and in mine it's 2026. But listen, how old are you?'

'I'm forty-one,' he said, and she could see he wondered why she was asking.

'No, I mean, how old are you here and now? Are you forty-one or thirty-eight?'

He chuckled. 'Shit, you're funny,' he said after studying her face for a moment. 'That was quick! I'm pretty certain I'm still forty-one.'

With bowls of cereal and a rack of toast on the table they settled down to breakfast and Abigail had a change of heart. It would probably be better to wait for Harry to bring things up rather than asking questions, and sooner or later he would revert to that strange incident at the airport he had mentioned earlier. She had a strong feeling that more detail would emerge if she let things develop randomly instead of asking questions, however much she wanted to voice the ever growing list of queries in her mind.

'Your computer,' said Harry and reached for the plum jam. 'What was it you called it?'

For a moment she was confused. 'I think I just said I'd get my laptop.'

'Is that what you call a portable?'

'Yes, we call it laptop because you don't need a table you can put it on your lap.' She had never thought of it before and was struck by how odd this was. We get used to a phrase, she thought, and we stop noticing what it really means. Portable is a much better word.

Harry pushed his chair back and got to his feet with his mug in his hand and started talking very fast, leaning back against the kitchen bench. 'This is what happened. What I think caused this ... time malfunction. There was a strange event at Auckland airport while I was waiting for my connecting flight - a tremendous crack, like a bomb going off, and all the lights went out. The whole place went silent, and when the lights came on again we just stared at each other, nearly deafened by the noise. My ears were ringing, and a woman next to me was bent forward holding her hands to her temples as if her head hurt.'

He took a sip of his coffee and appeared lost in thought for a moment. 'And then they made an announcement over the speaker system and said the airport building had been struck by lightning, but the thunder would soon move on and there was no risk to anybody, but some of their systems were down and would need to be restarted. And then, just a moment later it happened again, another deafening crack but much louder this time – the whole building shook. People's faces were screwed up in pain, the sound was like a physical assault. It was terrifying.'

He went back to his chair and sat down, as if now that he had told her the start of the story he could relax again. 'But the strangest thing,' he said and kept his eyes fixed on hers, 'is what happened next. A huge glowing ball of lightning rolled down the entire length of the terminal, some people were knocked off their feet. I threw myself to one side, because I could see it was coming straight for me, but I can't have got my arm out of the way - it must have touched my arm as it rolled past. The next thing I remember is waking up in the snow outside this house, freezing cold and totally confused.'

'A ball of lightning? Is there such a thing? I've never heard of it before.'

'Oh yes, ball lightning, it's a well-known phenomenon. Not common, but it's been documented many times. I don't know quite what causes it, why it forms into a ball, but it's a highly concentrated mass of electric energy. Very high voltage and it seems to move on a straight path, quite unlike the lightning we see in the sky. I think I remember reading about a ball of lightning rolling down the aisle in a passenger plane a few years ago when they flew through a thunderstorm.'

'So, it burnt you,' said Abigail. 'It touched your arm as it rolled past and made that mark. But it doesn't look fresh, it's not a wound like a fresh burn would be, it looks like an old scar.'

He smiled grimly and lifted his coffee mug as if in a toast. 'Well, there you go, another mystery to solve. An injury that happened three years from now in another time, which had resolved itself into a scar when I was flicked back to 2026. It doesn't make sense, but then nothing about this whole thing makes much sense, does it?'

9

After a long silence Abigail started clearing the table. 'Let's do some research,' she said over her shoulder as she put the dishes in the dishwasher. 'Let's see what we can find out about you in this timestream. We need to get a handle on a couple of things first up - like do you exist in this city right now, so are you risking meeting yourself in the street one day and causing total confusion?'

He picked up the sponge from beside the basin and wiped the table. 'Can we have another cup of coffee while we do this, please?'

'Of course, just fill the kettle and make us each a cup. I have milk and half a sugar. I just need to go to the bathroom before I have any more coffee.'

With Harry sitting beside her Abigail clicked on the Firefox shortcut icon on her laptop screen and went straight to one of the major news sites. 'Let's have a look at the news first, just in case other people have materialised in random places - like outside the houses where they lived in 2029.'

'Excellent plan.' Harry gave her a wry smile. 'If that's the case we can stop worrying and I won't have to explain a thing. But it might just mean that others got transferred to another year, not 2026.'

There was nothing about unexplained appearances, but he pointed at one headline after another and asked Abigail to open the articles. After ten minutes of Harry reading random stories and making no comment, she turned to look at him, intrigued by the varied articles he had been reading. 'What are you looking for?'

'Nothing in particular, just trying to get grip what's going on, but some of it doesn't make sense.'

'How does it not make sense?' asked Abigail. 'Explain, please.'

'Some things they refer to,' he said. 'They never happened in my world. There's a reference to a devastating war between Israel and Gaza a couple of years ago that I've never heard of . And several mentions of climate change and global warming. I've never heard those terms, but I can imagine what they mean.'

Abigail was silent for a long moment staring vacantly at the laptop screen thinking about what he had just said, and gradually things slotted into a theory in her head.

'This proves what we talked about before, the timestream thing. The way we both own this house at the same time is just one thing that supports it.

You're not from my future. You're from a different timestream, a different dimension of time. Some kind of offshoot or sideline from this one we're in now. So if these things never happened in your timestream it must be because yours separated from this one *before* those events. We need to start looking at your connections and see if we can figure out when the split happened.' She thought for a moment, trying to sort this out in her mind and added. 'But, of course it might not be a *split*, maybe there have always been more than one timeline. Perhaps with a few things in common, some things happening in one and not in another. Maybe there are lots of them in parallel, but slightly out of sync?'

The only sound in the kitchen was the ticking on the wall clock while they stared at each other, as if neither of them could believe what she had just said. Finally, Harry broke the silence. 'You know what this means, don't you? If the split as you call it happened before my date of birth, I might not exist here at all.'

Abigail nodded. 'Crazy, isn't it? That's why I think it's important to find out if it *is* a split and from what date. Let's check your family history because that might tell us something. If there are multiple timestreams going on at different speeds with some things in common, we need to establish if you exist in the here and now. I mean, apart from you sitting in my kitchen after being moved from one timestream to this one.'

Then she laughed and said, 'You'll have to excuse

me if I sound incoherent at times, but this is all so weird and so hard to get a grip on. It's like living in a sci-fi novel where anything could happen. I can't believe I'm taking this so calmly – perhaps we're both delusional.'

The troubled look was back on his face, there was no trace of their light-hearted exchange of a few minutes ago. 'And then? I'm here in your timestream, where I don't belong, but am I still also in my timestream? Do I exist in two places at the same time?'

All she could say was, 'I have no idea. We'll have to try to work it out, but I can't imagine how we could prove if you exist here and there simultaneously. But admit it doesn't seem likely that you got *physically* moved over, does it? Wouldn't it be more reasonable to think you got kind of cloned into this timestream, like a copy? But right now, I think it might be more useful to try to identify the point in time where your timestream and mine split apart, if that's what happened. That way we'll know if you're at risk of being challenged by someone – some relative perhaps.' She frowned as another thought popped into her head, 'What's your surname? I need to know your full name and your date of birth to search for you on the Internet.'

'Hipkins,' he said, and Abigail typed it in, only just managing to hold in the comment that had been on the tip of her tongue. There was probably no point saying, 'like that Prime Minister', because Harry might not know who Chris Hipkins was.

A raft of suggested links appeared on her screen, and she scrolled slowly down until she realised that there were far too many and went back to the search bar and added "New Zealand geologist" to his name. She put quotation marks around the words to indicate that she only wanted to see entries that had all those words, and the result was more or less what she had expected, "no results featuring all those words".

'What now? Should we try someone you know or a relative? We have to find a starting point, something we can get hold of - something you recognise and then go from there.'

'Try my wife. Her name is Katrina with a K Hipkins. She's a nurse at the hospital here.'

She searched for Katrina by her full name with the added words "nurse" and "New Zealand" but the only New Zealand nurses called Katrina had the wrong surnames or lived in the wrong cities.

'Your parents - of course! We'll start with them and go forward.'

After a few minutes of searching and discarding various suggestions Harry identified his father, John Hipkins, from a wedding photograph taken when he married Christine Taylor in 1982. Harry had turned his chair half sideways to see the laptop, which was now at an angle, so they could both read the screen.

'That's not my mother,' he said with a strange look on his face. 'My mother's name is Diane, her maiden name was McLean, and they got married in 1986. '

Two parallel lines appeared between his eyebrows and his lips clamped together as if to stop himself saying something he would rather not. She said it for him: 'So this time split, happened before 1982 and in this timestream you've never existed.'

'I know, but what does it mean? Who am I, then?'

'You're still Harry, you've just been dislocated in time, kind of copied into this timestream. I think it's a good thing.' She was deeply relieved that Harry had never existed in her timestream and there would be no complications with family or relations. But now she must make sure he remained in this solid, calm state that he'd been in nearly since he woke up on the hall floor. His amazing composure was important for her own state of mind.

'Look at it from this point of view - it means you can't bump into yourself in the street, so you won't have to live locked in this house for the rest of your life.' She adopted a reasonable tone of voice and tried to look calm. 'And it avoids complications like not recognising your brother or your best mate.' He nodded but said nothing, so she continued. 'I know this sounds brutal, but we've got to face facts. You're stuck in 2026 in a branch of time that split off before your father married your mother, so you're safe from a whole raft of tricky issues.'

He shook his head, drank some coffee and gradually the desolate look on his face faded. 'You're right.' He managed a wry smile. 'Of course, it's much better from one point of view. I've lost my mother and my siblings and presumably my friends from 2029, but I'm not risking coming face to face with myself. On the other hand, I can't just appear here out of nowhere with no background and no connections, can I? I won't even have a PIC in this life.'

'Sorry,' said Abigail and put her hand briefly on his and wondered why he hadn't mentioned losing his wife, a strange omission. 'I'm really sorry! I was forgetting the people you've lost, your past achievements and how that feels. I was being simplistic and only considering what might go wrong.'

'You're being practical and very helpful - I want to thank you. I don't think many people would be prepared to do all these things you are doing for me. I was very lucky to find you living in my - I mean, in this house.'

Abigail smiled. 'What's a pic?'

'Don't you have PICs? It's short for personal identity card. You have to carry it with you, you can't do a thing without it, and the police have the right to demand you show it – anytime and anywhere - to prove who you are. They carry scanners so they can record where you are when they ask for it.'

'We have various forms ID cards and things like passports and driver's licences we use if we need to prove who we are, but yours sounds different, regulated by law. So, you must carry it all the time?'

'Yeah, if you don't have it on you when someone asks for it you get a mark against your name, and if it happens more than once there's a penalty. They've been very strict about it since the Global Union of Nations decided that all countries should use the same formalities and have the same regulations. Here's an example – when I went to Brazil I showed it in the taxi, at all airports I passed through, in the taxi in Rio de Janeiro, at my hotel – over and over. I can't access my bank account, log on to my portable or any computer, or purchase a vehicle without it.' He yawned and rubbed his eyes. 'If you don't have a valid PIC in my world you won't survive, not unless you're prepared to sleep in a cave and live on plants and fish or something.'

10

'Are you tired?' Abigail watched exhaustion slowly reclaiming Harry's face and wondered how many more disturbing discoveries he could cope with at this rapid pace of progress. His life had been turned upside down, he had no identity and no idea about what his future might turn into. And all that on top of nearly freezing to death and collapsing on her hall floor.

'Why don't you lie down for a while, even if you don't sleep, just have a rest. You've been through so much and your whole system must be in shock, physical and mental.

After a short discussion that nearly turned into a debate, he reluctantly agreed to lie down on the sofa in the living room "for a short rest" and Abigail said she would sit in her usual chair and read for a while.

'Just to keep you company,' she said breezily, as if this was something she would do for any random visitor. She hoped he would fall asleep and get some proper rest, and she wanted to be right there in the same room, prepared to intervene if he had a sudden melt-down. It wouldn't be surprising, she thought, and silently marvelled at how composed he had been so far. Just occasional moments when he looked sad and once really devastated, but mostly OK. A strong mind, she concluded, a man with a high level of composure and self-control, not given to emoting about what can't be changed. She tried to put herself in his situation and shuddered at the image it conjured up in her mind of panicking and crying, losing control, definitely not composed.

Within a few minutes of putting his head on one of the cushions he was deeply asleep, his face relaxed and the creases between his eyebrows smoothed out. This was the first time since he lay unconscious in the dimly lit hall that she could really study him. A handsome man with straight eyebrows a shade darker than his brown hair, a beautiful mouth and a strong chin. Even in his sleep his hand rested on his lower arm, as if he could still feel the shock of being hit by the ball lightning.

After a while she had an idea and went to the little desk in the corner of the living room where she often sat with her laptop, where she could see the garden through the terrace doors while writing emails or reading online news.

With her notebook beside her and a pen in hand she was soon lost in thought as she tried to work out what her priorities should be. Probably the most important thing was to establish an identity for Harry. Something credible and provable; the kind of things you need to have to get a passport or a driver's licence or to simply open a bank account. If he remained in her time, he must either take on the identity of somebody who had died, or if that proved impossible, masquerade as someone who didn't need either a passport or a driver's licence. It might be possible for Harry to live without formal ID, provided he never had to go to hospital or see a doctor, and if he didn't need a driver's licence, but eventually something would trip him up and then he would have to explain – and who would believe him?

Her phone buzzed in the kitchen, and she ignored it, because she had just had another idea and started a list of websites and topics Harry must read to catch up on recent history. He would flounder in a lot of contexts if he didn't have a good grasp of recent events and key events of international significance from the last ten or twenty years. Then she thought of social media and wondered why her search for his family hadn't started with Facebook. Such an obvious choice, but now that they knew he had never been born in this timestream it was no longer important. His father might have sons, who looked exactly like him, but that needn't worry them – everyone had a doppelganger, as they say. The fact that she hadn't even thought of social media earlier showed how the situation had impacted on her, thrown such a curve ball into her normally orderly world that some things simply hadn't occurred to her.

She walked across to check on Harry, who was deeply asleep and didn't react when she covered his legs with the rug she had put over him in the night. The recollection of how slow his heartbeat had been made her feel it was important to keep him warm.

So, on and on, while Harry slept, Abigail continued speculating, building theories and constructing scenarios that might be helpful. He needed a new identity, but nobody could exist in today's society without a credible back story. Her mind spawned vague ideas and discarded most of them as too simplistic or prone to complications, and yet another page in the notebook was devoted to half-formed ideas. The most important thing was to invent a credible explanation for why he had no birth record, because everything in life started with that crucial database of Births, Deaths and Marriages, from where everyone's life could be traced and proven. Her experience as an administrator at the Court meant she knew a lot of things most people wouldn't know, and one of those things was that it was no longer possible to simply steal a dead baby's identity the way people had done for criminal purposes until a couple of decades ago. But maybe a birth certificate from some other country?

She fetched her laptop, opened a new document and started organising her scribbled notes into a set of lists with headings and in the order she felt they should be tackled to avoid back-tracking. Soon her handwritten notes began to make logical sense with a brief paragraph alongside each bullet point explaining the reasoning behind her opinion, and gradually a well-constructed a map of ways forward took shape but with many question marks. When Harry stirred and then sat up looking groggy, as if he wasn't sure of where he was, she had just checked the time and decided to make lunch.

11

When she suggested an early lunch because how early they had breakfast, he expressed no enthusiasm but agreed it was a good idea. She closed the notebook and flicked down the lid of her laptop, not prepared to go into details about what she had been doing. So far Harry had been amazingly accepting of his situation, but he might be overwhelmed, not only by her extensive list of things that needed looking into, but also of the explanations that might be needed.

'We could go for a drive so you can check what's different now.' She hesitated. 'But it might be a bit risky if we come across someone I know or have to stop for some reason. I could just say you're my friend Harry, but what if they ask where you're from or something? If you invent something we might get into trouble later if we need to change it. Maybe we'd better leave the drive for later.'

He thought about this for a moment, then he nodded. 'OK, that makes sense. What were you writing?' His eyes slid to her laptop, and she realised he had noted how quickly she closed the lid when he approached her little desk.

'I'm compiling a list of things we need to think about,' she said casually, picked up the laptop and led the way to the kitchen. 'You know, how we might find out more about when your timestream split off, if that's what it did, and how to establish a new identity for you, that kind of thing. And I was pondering a few other problems that cropped up while you slept. Let's go through them in detail later. We'll have plenty of time a couple of weeks from now.'

'What's happening then?'

'I have a week's leave, not this coming week but the next one, and the HR department told me I have too much leave building up, so I could take another week after that. You'll be able to stay here while I'm at work for five days, and you can use my laptop and do what you like in the way of research, and then the following week we can both work on what you want to explore further. We'll have lots of time to do it – and plenty of time for getting sidetracked, which I'm pretty sure we will be.'

Over lunch they reverted to the discussion about timestreams and how they might be linked. 'I was reading something recently,' said Abigail with her fork full of scrambled egg suspended over her plate and noticed his eyes fixed on the fork. 'An article about the time-space continuum and a theory that there might be untold duplicates of our universe. This puzzle of ours with parallel timestreams seems to be on vaguely similar lines, but how anyone would prove or disapprove it I can't even imagine. Probably impossible.'

'You're right about not going for a drive,' said Harry unexpectedly. 'I'd rather start finding out more about your list of things to consider. Let's do the most important things first.' He gave her a glance of sly glee. 'You just mentioned the drive to keep me calm, didn't you? Something normal to take the tension out of the situation and stop me worrying?'

It made her laugh inside, that look. He had understood her motivation and enjoyed letting her see it.

'Yep,' she said calmly. 'And one-nil to you! You're obviously far more resilient than I thought. You just looked a little less composed than before, when you woke up from your nap. But don't misunderstand me, I can't believe how calm you are. I tried to imagine myself in your situation, and I'm sure I'd be lying in a heap on the floor sobbing.'

'Ha! Not you!' was all he said. After lunch he went upstairs to the bathroom and Abigial started putting things in the dishwasher, but when he returned his exclamation of surprise made her look up. 'Is that what dishwashers still look like here? Interesting! I didn't notice it before. I've seen these in old houses a couple of times, but I didn't know what they look like inside.'

'And? What do yours look like? There's not much you can change about a dishwasher, is there?'

He gestured at the folded down door with one rack pulled out. 'We gave up on those inconvenient things decades ago. Imagine if you didn't have to have that huge door folded down impeding traffic in the kitchen, and if you didn't have to go through a second move to pull out the rack or shelf or whatever you call it.' He had that mischievous look on his face again, he was enjoying this.

A little game, she thought and pretended to be offended. 'And how would you get around that then? Suspend it from the ceiling and open the door mid-air?'

'Two deep drawers,' he said and used his hands to sketch the outlines on the cupboards under the bench. 'Both independently powered and plumbed. Pull one out, load stuff into it and start it when it's full, then start filling the bottom one if you need it. Perfect solution. Open and close one thing, no need to have that awful door blocking so much space in a kitchen.'

Abigail smiled with malicious enjoyment and said innocently, 'Oh, you mean *dish drawers*! I was thinking of replacing this monster with two of those soon – it takes me too long to fill the dishwasher and for some silly reason I hate running it half full. The drawers would be far more practical.'

'Ha!' he said again, they both laughed.

'Let's look at the first list.' Abigail pulled the laptop closer and pointed to the chair beside her. 'Sit beside me again so we can both see it. These are things I think you need to know before you interact with anyone but me, background stuff. The first part is a list of key things from the last forty years, just outlines and each one followed by a hyperlink to a web page with more details, and that last one is a link a website that lists events of importance where you can look up specific decades. I only found that one right at the end.'

She scrolled down to the next page and pointed. 'This is link to a very good site with current vocabulary, recent slang, terms used on social media and abbreviations, like those people use when texting. That's not urgent, but it will probably be useful sooner or later.'

'Stop! You lost me there. Texting? What's texting? And social media? Some kind of news place? And those links, whatever you called them – hyperlinks?'

'Oh God, I'm sorry!' Suddenly she realised what a mammoth task this was going to be for Harry, a huge education plan of facts and references to things that he would then have to look up, an endless flow of one thing leading to another. 'This is going to be a steep learning curve – I hadn't quite taken in how it must seem to you. I'll have to think about how to go about it. There's so much you need to catch up with if you're going to be able to function.'

'Oh, I know, don't panic,' he said, as if to comfort her and once again his confidence and calm struck her as extraordinary. She watched him for a moment, the serious brown eyes looking back at her and then that little tweak at the corner of his mouth, the nearly hidden amusement.

'What's funny? I wasn't really panicking, I just felt guilty that maybe I was overwhelming you.' She gave him a wry smile. 'I'm often accused of being a compulsive list-maker, too organised for most people.'

'Not for me,' said Harry. 'I'm highly organised myself, methodical in most things, so it's all good. But explain those things you mentioned – and don't forget the hyperlinks. Such an interesting word.'

They spent an hour investigating social media and getting sidetracked into discussions and explanations that Harry's questions brought up.

'So, there are people who deliberately manufacture fake news just to … what? Trick people, upset them? I can't see the point.' He frowned and thought for a moment. 'And with this fantastic wealth of facts and background information available to verify things – don't people research things, look things up for themselves?'

'Most don't,' said Abigail briefly, as always appalled at the spread of misinformation. 'I'm afraid too many people are gullible and ready to believe anything that sounds like a scandal or something a politician or some famous person is trying to hide. It excites them, and then they share it, and somehow it starts taking on a veneer of truth instead of rumour. But don't you have a version of the internet? You seem surprised at how much there is to find.'

'Ours is very limited compared to this, no so-called social media. The authorities keep strict tabs on what's published – in book form or on what you call the internet.' He gave her that wry smile she was getting very familiar with, the one that said what he felt as clearly as spoken words. 'We have websites where government officials distribute information and people can ask questions, but you don't always get an answer. It's the same everywhere, in every country. It's never occurred to me that it could be like this – for anyone to use with no restrictions.'

Abigail shook her head. 'Far more totalitarian than what we have here, even in countries like China. Maybe North Korea would be the closest to what you describe. But let's go back to hyperlinks – they appear in blue in my list, and you click on them like this with the Ctrl button held down at the same time, see?'

'And there it is. What a great tool. Can I try?'

'You saw how I scrolled up and down the page? Find a hyperlink you're interested in and try it yourself.' She smiled as he pulled the laptop to a better angle and used the hyperlinks, one after the other, like someone with a new toy.

'I'm going to really enjoy this,' he said after ten minutes of going back and forth and reading a bit here and there. 'That place that lists major events per decade is great – very convenient.'

By the end of the day, they were mentally exhausted and ate their dinner without talking much, both immersed in their own thoughts. Abigail said she'd go upstairs after Harry on the excuse that she wanted to make sure all doors and windows were locked, but what she really wanted to do was check the security footage again, particularly the time just before and after when Harry materialised on the front lawn. The thought that someone might have seen him, as he lay on the ground or when he walked naked to her front door, worried her. That morning, when she first looked at it, she had been concentrating first on Harry and then on the lack of footprints in the snow, but now the risk of someone having seen him was at the top of her mind.

She sat at the kitchen table, so deep in concentration that she didn't hear Harry come downstairs again.

'What are you doing?' he said, and she jumped. 'Shouldn't you go to bed? You've been up more or less a day and a half.'

She sat up straight and stretched her arms over

her head. 'I'm watching the footage from the outside camera. In case someone was watching your … arrival. I don't want any surprises.'

Once again he pulled out the chair beside her and she angled the laptop, so he could see. 'I'll go back to the start again, but I think it's OK. I'll play it at normal speed.'

Together they studied the peaceful scene lit by the streetlamp: little snowflakes gently falling, no traffic and nothing moving. The light snow cover on the lawn was an unbroken white carpet and then Snap! there was a body, a naked man curled up in the centre of the lawn, and no footprints to or from where he lay. After a couple of minutes he got onto his hands and knees, then stood. With his back to the camera he looked around, turned towards the house and made his way to the front door, unsteady and visibly shivering, leaving footprints from his bare feet in the snow.

'I've checked twice,' said Abigail and ran her hands through her hair. 'There are no houses across the road, just the park and the playground. No pedestrians and no cars. It was so lucky I had the camera on continuous recording. My neighbours to the left, whose house is closer to the street than mine, they could have seen you from their kitchen window, but they're away on holiday. I think we're safe.'

'It's incredible, isn't it? The way you can see I don't fall to the ground - I materialise out of nowhere. Would anyone but us believe it or would they think it was a hoax?'

There was no answer; she shook her head and turned the laptop off.

12

After lying awake for a long time Abigail fell asleep with questions still revolving in her mind and without having come up with any new ideas about how to create a new identity for Harry. There must be some way of doing both that and give him a credible back story, so he could at least superficially be acceptable as genuine, even if they couldn't prove in any formal way who he was.

She woke up before dawn and lay there for a moment slightly confused looking at the soft light coming in through her half-open bedroom door. Of course! It was the little night light she had plugged in to the wall socket in the upstairs hall in case Harry got up in the night. She laughed at herself when she remembered that he was as familiar with the layout of the house as she was. Then out of nowhere she knew who could help them, and she couldn't believe she hadn't thought of him earlier. Jasper! The obvious choice, the only person she knew who might be able to do what had to be done. Jasper, who for the last dozen years had sent the same text message on the thirteenth of December, more or less word for word identical messages: *Once again, thank you for saving my skin and my career. And as always, if you ever need me just let me know. You kept your word, and I will keep mine, J*

I have that time off work coming up, she thought, and I think I need him here, face to face with Harry, if it's going to work. Between the three of us we should be able to do it. She reached for her phone on the bedside table, energised now and feeling upbeat she texted Jasper. *The day has come, and I need you here for at least a couple of days. If possible during the week after this coming one. Abigail xx*

Standing at the kitchen bench an hour later, suddenly and for no reason, the reality of Harry only having landed in her garden on Friday night and what had developed since suddenly struck Abigail as crazy. 'Unbelievable,' she said quietly to herself. 'Crazy!'

'What? Is something wrong?' Harry asked and she heard him push his chair back. She turned and pointed a finger at his chest which was now very close. 'Would you have believed this if it happened in your world? If I turned up on your doorstep stark naked in the middle of winter and claimed the house was mine?'

She realised instantly what she had said, but it was too late. Harry's eyes glinted with amusement.

'I wouldn't believe my luck! But seriously – it is crazy and as you said yesterday, it's impossible but it did happen. And the most amazing thing is that you've taken me in and will keep me safe.'

She looked seriously at him. 'But it's not just how we accepted the situation, is it? It's how much we achieved in one day, when I look back, I can't believe it. I just kind of lined it up in my head while I was waiting for the toaster, and it seems unreal that we got so far yesterday, got so much done.'

'Maybe we have that thing you were telling me about last night when I asked about movies – superpowers, wasn't it? I mean, what else could it be?'

Then the toast popped up behind her and Abigail laughed, put the toast on a plate and sat down at the table. 'And talking about extraordinary – don't leave out how you're coping and already leaning so much new stuff.'

All he said, while spreading peanut butter on a piece of toast, was, 'Maybe it's because how happy I am not to be in that dystopian world I came from, so I can't wait to learn how to live here. Did you think of that?'

That simple concept stopped her in her tracks. 'Oh God, I'm sorry, I didn't even think of what that must feel like. But you've lost so much, family and friends, and you might feel as if you have no connections now. You're very brave.'

Don't mention his wife! she reminded herself. She must leave the wife out of all conversations until he explained why he never mentioned her. There must be a strong reason for it, and the last thing she wanted to do was upset him. His incredible composure was not built on solid rock and keeping him emotionally balanced was important for them both.

'Of course I miss people, but not the way my world was – so restricted and controlled.' He looked serious now with intense focus on her, as if seeing her reactions was particularly important. 'But I have you, if I may put it that way and that's incredible – the greatest piece of luck ever. There might not be anyone else in the world who would handle it the way you have.' He smiled at her head shake. 'No, I mean it. Not to mention that you live alone and seem to be prepared to put up with me hiding out here for an indefinite time.'

She decided this conversation must stop right there. In the back of her mind a little voice warned her not to imagine he was interested in her on a personal level. That she found him very attractive meant nothing. It was a one-sided thing and better kept under wraps or their life in this house might become impossible. She must keep in mind that for now, what mattered most was to integrate Harry into normal life, enable him to do whatever he wanted to do and then kind of set him free. So what she said, instead of something utterly inappropriate, was, 'I've asked a friend from my past to come for a couple of days next week – a guy called Jasper. He owes me a huge favour and I'm calling it in.'

The expression that appeared on his face was gone so quickly that she would have missed it if she blinked, but she took note and continued smoothly, 'He's a guy I used to work with in Wellington. We worked for a government agency that deals with protecting sensitive data and communications, and a few other background things. A place most people have never heard of. I was there for three years, until Mike and I moved back here.' She took a sip of her coffee and watched him over the rim of her mug, thinking she had probably been mistaken about that look that flitted across his face earlier. 'Anyway, Jasper did something very, very bad, criminal. God knows what made him do it, he could never explain it afterwards – but anyway, I saved his job and his career, so he owes me.'

Harry was visibly curious now and started to say something but changed his mind and waited. 'So,' said Abigail and reached for the jam jar, 'because of his skills and training, and also his access to systems that are now out of my reach, I've decided to call in the favour.'

'Did nobody discover what he did? You totally fixed it?'

'What he did wasn't just stupid, it could have endangered the country's security and potentially that of other countries too. If it had been discovered he would have lost his job and been prosecuted, which would have ruined his future in the industry.' She smiled at the memory of those couple of fraught days while they waited to see if her subversive ploy had worked, the most suspense filled days in her life. 'He's an IT guy with very specialised skills – and he designed an improvement to our system and installed it without testing it in isolation first. And it turned out to be very dangerous. All I did was create a diversion, something quite devious and potentially troublesome, which drew the attention away and enabled him to restore things to the way they had been before he uploaded his patch, which saved both the overall situation and him.'

She could see that Harry was fascinated by the story. Something in it had connected and she knew enough about him by now to be able to guess how many questions he was lining up in his head.

'How did you do that?'

She smiled casually. 'Oh, you know, just blackmail and a bit of extortion – nothing special.'

Harry laughed outright. 'Ha! I knew it! I just knew there was a bit of naughty devilry inside that pragmatic front - I've been waiting for it to emerge. Was Jasper a boyfriend?'

Thinking of Jasper in the role of boyfriend nearly made her laugh. 'Oh no, just a very good friend. He's that lovely kind of gay man who really likes women and makes a fabulous confidante. I don't' see him often these days, only every couple of years, but every single year he texts me on the anniversary of this little drama and tells me he's ready to help when I need him. And that moment has finally come.'

'He's gay? As in homosexual – and openly? Is it legal?'

Aha, thought Abigail, here's another thing that makes our timestream so different. Maybe liberal attitudes never took root in his world. 'It's been legal for about fifty years, I think,' she said after thinking for a moment. 'At least – and there are many versions of what we could call non-standard sexuality. It's quite possible that Jasper is bi-sexual, not just gay, but I've never asked him. It doesn't matter, does it? Are you shocked?'

'Not at all! I was just surprised for a moment. The difference compared to where I come from is startling at times. Being found to be gay would mean a correction camp, and being discovered in a compromising situation means you get instantly arrested and not seen again for a long time, years, you just disappear. Some come back and have been cured, as they call it. Some men come back castrated.'

'What? That's terrible!'

He nodded. 'I know, but that's how it is, and it has been for as long as I can remember.'

Trying to assimilate this dystopian concept she watched Harry spread peanut butter on a second slice of toast and waited for the obvious question. After a moment he looked up. 'Is his visit about creating an identity for me? Could he do it? And more importantly, would he? Would it be safe for him to do it?'

'We'll have to explain the whole thing, of course,

but I promise you can trust him. He's got to be told everything, absolutely everything. Where you came from and how. That you have no background at all, so you need a whole fictional life created around you, not just a name and a date of birth. Plus the added complication of your degree and profession. You can't function in a vacuum. Let's face it, you just got beamed down from space like an alien in a sci-fi film, didn't you?'

Their eyes met and they both laughed, and Abigail thought for the second time this morning how nice it was to have someone to laugh with. They felt precious, these little instances of being in sync, a bit like what she had with Mike, but in a very different way.

'I'll sleep on the sofa while he's here, so he can have the guest room.' Harry nodded to himself. 'It's not as if I have a lot of belongings to shift.'

Pleased with how much Harry was eating, and how normal it seemed, Abigail got to up to put more bread in the toaster. 'He won't be staying here. I'll book him into a hotel. I've never liked having people sleeping on sofas, apart from a nap in the middle of the day.'

'What do you think about that sightseeing trip we talked about yesterday?' she asked when they had cleared the table. 'I know you're dying to sit down and start reading all the things I listed yesterday, but maybe a little road trip might be nice. I've thought about it and the risk of complications is probably minimal, but it's up to you.'

'Not yet,' he said decisively. 'But thank you for thinking of it. I'd rather not be seen until I have some credible background, something that sounds remotely sane, and I'd much rather start my study programme right away.'

'OK, let's leave it for now. I'll call Jasper this morning. And if you're going upstairs now, I'll come with you. For a start I need to give you a toothbrush and toothpaste – I do have spares. And I thought you could use Mike's electric shaver for the time being, if you don't mind a second-hand one. It's in one of those boxes I packed for the charity shop.' Abigail closed the dishwasher and wiped her hands. 'And we need to go through Mike's clothes and sort out anything that's too obviously something he used to wear – you know, things that people might recognise.'

'I hadn't thought of that. Let's go through the whole lot, so whatever I wear, in the house or outside, is anonymous and kind of generic.'

13

They emptied the boxes on floor in Harry bedroom and sorted them into piles on the bed. Everything that was distinctive and might be remembered as Mike's went back into boxes, but in the main his clothes turned out to be mostly the sort of things any man might own.

'Much like mine back in my world.' Harry studied the piles on the bed. 'We don't have that material you call fleece, but in the main it looks much like my own clothes.'

'Let's put everything that's OK for you to wear into the wardrobe and the chest of drawers.' Abigail contemplated what was now Harry's clothes. 'I think you'll have enough to see you through any kind of weather, but you're definitely going to need a new puffer jacket – Mike threw his out shortly before he was killed after he spilt tomato sauce on it when he was eating a hot dog in the car and then stain wouldn't come out. Shoes might be a problem.

You know how you sometimes have to buy a slightly different size depending on the shape of the shoes. Why don't you try everything in that carton full of shoes, and then we'll know what we need to get. Not that we can go shopping where I usually go – we'll have to go to some outlying suburb on the far side of town where I don't know anybody, if we need to get new shoes.'

'Enough to see me through for a while,' said Harry twenty minutes later, after trying on a dozen pairs of shoes and walking around in them to see how they felt before tossing nine pairs into the charity shop carton. 'One pair of very comfortable sneakers, one pair of seemingly unused loafers for indoors and a pair of boots in much the same state of newness – very smart boots, I like them. Did Mike decide they weren't comfortable or were they new when he died?'

He was looking carefully at her now, and she could guess what was in his mind; how would she react to the words "when he died".

'Oh no, they're not new,' she said calmly. 'I didn't even recognise those loafers at first when I was packing up all his things – he bought them years ago and I hadn't seen them since. But I think both those and the boots were bought without enough walking around in the shop – and then he discovered the boots gave him blisters, so they were never used. A bit too small for him, but perfect for you to step into.'

And then she realised what she had said, how

that phrase "step into" might sound in the context of shoes, as if she were telling Harry he was now stepping into Mike's place in her life, and she nearly moaned with frustration and felt herself blush. But Harry made no indication he had connected the dots, and Abigail's blush receded.

With the shoe problem resolved they headed for the stairs to return to the kitchen, but halfway down Abigail stopped. 'Hey, I know! I'll get Mike's laptop, and you can use it for your study project. I don't know why I didn't think of that earlier.'

'Here we are – I'll put it on the bench and plug it in,' said Abigail a few minutes later. 'It's not been turned on for months and the cord won't reach the table, and I can't find the extension cord.' She frowned and stared absently at the window. 'We did have one, it used to be rolled into a coil on the self in the coat cupboard in the hall, but … oh, I know where it is! I gave it to Astrid to take home one night when she was telling me how she can't have her radio alarm clock beside her bed because the wall socket is too far away.'

Straight away the "question mode" expression appeared on Harry's face. 'Who's Astrid?'

'She's my baby sister, much younger and sometimes a bit disorganised, but lovely. I'll tell you more about her later, perhaps tonight, but I must call Jasper now. I'll put the phone on speaker, so you can hear what he's like – such a great friend. He and Mike used to play chess together sometimes.'

With the phone on the table between them she

called Jasper, who sounded as if he was half asleep. 'Jesus, Abby – what time is it?'

'It's quarter to ten and we've been up for ages,' she said pleasantly. 'And good morning to you too, my friend! I just called to check which day you're planning to come, so I can book your air fare and a hotel.'

'Oh, for heaven's sake! I just woke up and read your text about five minutes ago, I had a very late night. I'll book things myself – there's no need for you to pay. I think I'll come down on Thursday the week after next and stay for the weekend ... or maybe fly back on the Saturday afternoon. I'll think about that. I'm not sure what's happening that weekend.'

'Aha, you have a new love in your life, do you? I haven't seen any significant photos on social media. Is he brand new?'

'No, just quite new - but he's married, so we're being careful until he's told his wife he's leaving.'

Abigail kept her eyes on Harry's face, not wanting to miss his expressions. This would be such a revelation to him. 'Wife as in woman wife or man wife?'

'Christ, Abby! You sound like my mum sometimes. That's exactly what she would ask – not that she knows about this new possible life partner. But his wife is a woman wife. Anything else you want to know?'

'I'm sure I'll think of a few things before you get here, but right now I just want to say we've been ...'

Jasper interrupted and now his voice turned serious. 'Who's we? A new man? And what's this problem you need help with, anyway? Must be serious if you're asking for help.'

'I have an unexpected visitor, and we're stuck with a problem that I can't see how to fix, but you might. I won't tell you more right now, you'll have to wait. It's a very long story, quite complex. I'll forward the air ticket to you and please take a taxi straight here when you arrive. Let me know what you want for dinner – I know your life revolves around food.'

'Let me tell you, I haven't put on a single kilo since you saw me last – I've been very restrained. But OK, I look forward to seeing you … both. Look after yourself, girl!'

'Will he believe it?' asked Harry when she ended the call. 'Maybe nobody but you will, it's such a mad thing. I hardly believe it myself.'

Abigail grinned. 'I have a great plan for how to do this. When he arrives we'll sit him down with a cup or a glass of something – and by the way, I must buy some beer, he doesn't drink wine. And then we play him the footage from the outside camera and watch his reactions. How could he *not* believe it?'

Once again they shared a smile before Abigail's phone gave its three-note alert of an incoming call and she had Astrid on the line. 'You know that guy you told me about once? The one who was often Mike's partner on jobs? What's his name?'

'You mean Aaron? Did you meet him somewhere?'

'Yeah, that's him. I was introduced to him at the funeral, but I'd forgotten his name. He came into the library yesterday morning, you know how we're open from ten to two on a Saturday. I had to go in to fill in for someone, who was sick. Anyway, he asked after you in a kind of funny way.'

Abigail made a face at Harry, who could hear the whole conversation because she had unthinkingly put her finger on the speaker button again. 'What exactly does that mean? A funny way?'

'Well,' said Astrid slowly. 'I'm not sure how to describe it, but he was kind of round-about and I think he was trying to find out if you were seeing someone without asking directly, and then he went a bit further and said you and he must take me out for dinner soon. Which was *weird* because you haven't said anything about dating him. But I don't like him, he looks like a bully to me, and he sounded devious somehow, so I said if he wanted to know anything about your life he'd better ask you, not me.'

Abigail laughed. 'You're such a staunch little sister – well done! And just so you know, I don't like him either and he's been a bit of a pest, so thanks for doing that!'

Now was not the time to answer the questions she felt sure were lining up in Harry's head, so when the call ended she put the phone to one side and said, 'Let's start up the other laptop now and I'll check how much charge it has, and if it's enough you can use it. If not, you can use mine while I do some other things.'

She got up and added with her back turned, ignoring the look she had caught on Harry's face, which was a ramped up version of the question mode look, 'I know you want to ask dozens of questions about Aaron, but we'll postpone that until tonight if you don't mind. Now it's learning time.'

Telling him the details about Aaron's pursuit of her could wait until she had decided how much she would tell him, because a strong streak of protectiveness was beginning to become obvious in her interactions with Harry. And though it was very different from Mike's attitude to her safety, the last thing she would allow would be for Harry to act in her defence and risk his own safety.

14

A couple of hours later Abigail was chopping an onion for a lunchtime omelette when she cut her forefinger quite badly. 'Oh shit!' She quickly pulled her hand away from the onion before blood dripped on it. Clamping her thumb over the cut to hold it shut she turned to Harry who was sitting in front of her laptop at the table. 'Can you please pass me a piece of kitchen paper, so I don't get blood everywhere – I must have cut very deep.'

Harry came over to look at her hand where blood was now dripping into the sink. 'Very deep,' he said. 'Here, wrap this around it really tight and keep your thumb on it while I'll run upstairs and get some sticking plasters. I presume they're in your bathroom? I don't think you should risk walking on the carpet.'

He had no sooner disappeared upstairs than there was a loud knock on the door, and Abigail knew without looking that Aaron would be standing on the doorstep. He never used the doorbell when he came to pick Mike up, and neither had he used it when he called after Mike's death. She went to the front door with her right hand cupped under her left to catch any drops of blood, managed with some difficulty to open the door and stood back. This was the first time he had come to the door for some time, and she didn't really want to see him, but blood was trickling into her cupped hand, and she couldn't stand there for long.

'Come into the kitchen,' she said, turned from the door and hoped that she would be able to get rid of him before Harry came down. 'I've just cut myself, and I don't want to stand here dripping blood on the carpet.'

Why on earth had she even let him in, she wondered and led the way to the kitchen while she tried to balance her hand so blood wouldn't spill. Why hadn't she simply ignored his knock and pretended she wasn't at home?

Aaron followed and stood undecided looking at the bloodstained paper around her hand. 'Is there anything I can do?'

'No thanks, it's under control. What can I do for you?'

Without warning he reached for her as if to hug her and said, 'You poor thing,' but Abigail took a rapid step back. 'No, Aaron, I don't need a hug - I'm not a five-year-old.'

'Mike would have wanted it, you know,' he said. 'Us together, I mean. He'd want you to be happy and have someone in your life - he would have approved of you and me together, and we're such a good fit.'

'*No*, Aroon,' said Abigail firmly. '*Stop!* We're not a good fit and I'm not in the least attracted to you, not in any way.'

She had never realised quite how insensitive he was, but now she could see he wasn't going to take no for an answer. His perverse determination to have his way overrode her protest. Then, just as he reached for her again, she saw a tiny movement through the kitchen door. Harry was standing halfway down the stairs, poised as if waiting for her to notice him. Now he started bouncing down the stairs in that athletic way he had, and she realised that he must have come down halfway and listened to the conversation without making a sound. A second later he appeared in the kitchen holding three sticking plasters. Aaron's eyes widened in surprise, and he took a step back as Harry approached Abigail.

'Sorry, mate,' said Harry casually. 'I think we've got to fix this before the introductions. It's bleeding quite a lot.'

They all looked at Abigail's forefinger wrapped in blood soaked paper that dripped slowly. 'Come here, honey,' said Harry and gripped her wrist and pulled her closer the sink. 'Let me see how bad it is.'

Aaron watched in silence, and by the look on his face Abigail knew he was as stunned as she was. It seemed that Harry had a plan, and she couldn't wait to hear what he'd come out with next.

Harry dropped the blood-soaked paper in the sink and studied the cut which was still trickling blood at a steady rate. 'I'll wrap these three sticking plasters really tight around it for now and then tonight we'll take them off and clean up the mess - get that cut closed up a bit more tightly, so it heals nicely.'

He applied the plasters and curled his fingers around hers, and a current of sudden and unexpected desire flowed up Abigail's arm. Lifting her hand he kissed her knuckles before he reached for the wad of bloodied paper in the sink, put it in the rubbish bin and turned back to rinse and dry his hands.

'Sorry about that, but first things first,' he said and turned to Aaron. 'I'm Harry.'

The look on Aaron's face was a mix of anger and confusion, but he pulled himself together and held out his hand. 'Aaron Tapper, I was a colleague of Mike's.'

To Abigail's quiet amazement Harry's performance continued seamlessly and without hesitation. 'Ah, yes - I remember Mike talking about you once, some story about a job you were on together.'

'So, you knew Mike? I don't think he ever mentioned you.'

Harry chuckled. 'Well, there's probably no reason why he'd mention a personal friend at work.

We met on holiday about four years ago. I was sorry I had to miss Mike's funeral, or we might have met there.'

Abigail saw her chance to contribute more credibility to the story and grabbed it. 'Five years ago,' she corrected untruthfully. 'In Arrowtown. Four years ago we went skiing together and stayed in Wanaka. And now you're here.' She smiled affectionately at Harry. 'Which is so nice instead of the long distance commuting.'

A couple of minutes later, having declined Harry's offer of coffee, Aaron left, and Abigail returned from closing the front door behind him, sat down at the kitchen table and burst into peels of helpless laughter. 'My God, you're a good actor! Had you been listening from the stairs before you came down?'

Harry grinned. 'I was at the top of the stairs when you opened the front door, so I heard the whole thing, and I could tell from the tone of your voice that you weren't happy to see him, but I didn't know why to start with – but that became clear, of course. I hope you didn't mind.'

'Mind? God no, I'm delighted. Such a perfect act to put him off his stride. He's one of two guys, who I think have heard that Mike had taken out that enormous life insurance policy. They think I'm worth having now.'

Harry looked searchingly at her and moved his head slowly from side to side. 'Is that a comment about you not being attractive? You said something similar earlier, but I don't understand what you mean. You're a very attractive woman. Who's been saying nasty things to you?'

'Oh, it's not what anyone said, but I'm well aware that I'm too chubby.' Abigail gave him a wry smile. 'I might have a reasonable face, but my body isn't that hot, so I always knew the manoeuvres from these two guys had nothing to do with me as a person. Aaron has never liked me. He's a misogynist and a woman who has opinions of her own doesn't fit with his world view.' She was silent for a moment before she added quietly. 'I'm pretty sure this crazy pursuit isn't based on attraction, all about the money and how much he'd like to have access to all it can buy.'

Harry made no response, just studied her silently as if he was trying to figure out if she was serious. She got up before this conversation could go any further, not ready to continue a discussion so personal and potentially upsetting.

'I'll make us another cup of coffee, and we'll have some of those coconut biscuits you liked. We can have a proper lunch a bit later, when I feel like tackling that onion again.'

Talking about her looks made her very uncomfortable. Mike had often said that there was nothing better than a pretty woman, who was also a cuddly armful in bed, but she had never quite believed that he really preferred her that way.

She was getting clean mugs out when Harry spoke behind. 'I can't imagine where this lack of belief in your looks comes from, but you couldn't be more wrong. You've got a pretty face and wonderful hair, and curves in all the right places - personally I can't think of anything nicer.'

She made no comment, just put the biscuit on the table and poured them mugs of coffee. Harry reached across and briefly put his hand on hers, and once again she felt that current run up her arm, just like when he touched her to put the sticking plasters on. They said nothing more about it and reverted to discussing things he had found online that had caught his interest.

After dinner on Sunday night Harry brought up Aaron's visit again, clearly intent on finding out more. 'I'd like to know a bit more about that Aaron guy,' he said casually as he stood by the kitchen bench pouring them each another glass of wine. 'And by the way – are we drinking you out of house and home, as they say? Too much?' He put the glass in front of Abigail and studied her face for a moment.

'If ever two people needed alcohol to deal with things it's us two right now,' said Abigail. 'I don't mean just this very moment, but until we feel a bit more in control. And I don't think a couple of standard glasses a day, like two thirds of a bottle between two of us, is excessive.'

Having considered the options she had decided that she must explain about Aaron, or Harry would be inventing various theories and perhaps even think there had been some kind of relationship between them.

'I'll tell you about Aaron,' she said as soon as Harry sat down opposite her. 'He was Mike's partner on and off for years, and when we went out for a drink with Mike's colleagues he made it very clear he didn't like women who have opinions.' She thought for a minute. 'And it wasn't just having opinions, perhaps what really got to him was that I could defend my opinions, I had looked things up, done a bit of research and sometimes proved him wrong. Which isn't the natural order of things as far as Aaron's concerned. Once, not long before Mike died, he made a very dismissive comment about blondes, which was clearly aimed at me. Not just dismissive - it also included a nasty little hint about what he thinks blond women were made for. Lucky for him that Mike didn't hear it.'

Harry's expression remained neutral, but she sensed a tension behind the facade. 'You said something about an insurance payout. I presume Mike had insured his life?'

She nodded. 'When Aaron turned up on my doorstep a while after Mike's death and asked me out, I turned him down – I'd already turned him down when he called and asked me to go to the movies earlier. He tried again, then he a sent flowers and then a present. But the creepiest thing was the card that came with the flowers, which said that he and I must pick up where we had left off! As if we had anything that could be picked up!

She took a sip of her wine and imagined she could nearly feel that horrible sensation of being stalked like prey by a predator. 'I knew there could only be one reason for his campaign of pretend affection, and I really felt uneasy. The way he comes across, his insensitivity and how determined he is to have his way, it's intimidating. You see, Mike had insured his life for millions and arranged for the premium to be paid by his lawyer. I never knew about it until after he died. He told Rob – that's our lawyer – that he wanted me to have a lovely surprise if he was killed.'

'And then Aaron found out about it somehow.' Harry nodded to himself. 'And he decided it was a great opportunity for him. Did someone in the lawyer's office tell him, do you think?'

'That's exactly what I thought too, and the way he came to the house in the evening, after dark and then the flowers and the present the sent – it felt as if he was stalking me, so I had a chat with Rob, and he recommended upgrading the security system and logging everything Aaron did. I might have over-reacted, but I felt hunted, like prey – very uncomfortable.'

'You know that cheese we had last night?' said Harry with a surprising change of topic. 'Is there some left, and if there is, can we have it now with the rest of the wine? I really liked it, a kind I hadn't come across before.'

Intervention, thought Abigail, and smiled inside. He heard my voice change a bit there and thought he would de-escalate the slight tension I betrayed. He's very alert to things like that. 'Of course, I just didn't think of it – and there's another cheese you might like too, a Danish camembert style cheese I buy sometimes. I'll get both out if you get the box of crackers from the pantry.'

With the after dinner treat between them, Abigail put a slice of camembert on a wholemeal cracker and continued the story. 'So the security system software is up-to-date now, and I have the app on my phone, so I can see who's outside whether I'm at home or not. I have it on my laptop too, as you saw, so I can save portions of footage as evidence. You know, shots Aaron sitting outside in his car watching the house or driving very slowly past and looking at the house. Rob said all these things could make the case stronger if I need to get a restraining order against him some time in the future.'

'Are you scared of him becoming physically aggressive? I could tell you hated him touching you – from where I was on the stairs I saw your expression when he tried to take hold of you.'

"Oh no, I'm not scared of him physically. Even if he lost his temper with me for telling him to back off, I don't think he'd hurt me. Not seriously, anyway, but he might try a bit harder, push his way inside, maybe try to get me into a position where he could kiss me - or something worse.'

Harry made no direct comment, just said calmly,

'Let's hope the fact that I'm here has made it clear that it's pointless for him to try.'

Abigail laughed at the memory of Harry putting the plasters on her finger. 'I think your act with my cut finger convinced him. He was literally stunned when you appeared and took over – and so was I.'

Harry smiled at the memory. 'And then you fed into the story so cleverly and corrected me about how long it was since we first met, that was brilliant, it made the whole thing totally convincing. He'll probably never come back. Or if he does, I'll deal with him.'

'How would you deal with him?' Various scenarios played out like little video clips in Abigail's head, some of them a bit risky. 'You wouldn't tackle him physically, would you? He's known as a bully at the station, and he probably knows how to fight.'

'So do I.' Harry's smile was relaxed and confident. 'I'm a very good fighter, even if I've never used it in a so-called situation before. I've been going to a boxing and kung fu club since I was a teenager, so I can at least defend you – and myself.'

'Aha! So that's where those biceps and the big shoulders came from. I noticed when I was trying to drag you in the door, so I could wrap you up. Very impressive, but it made it hard to get a grip on your upper arms.'

'Enough of this talk about me helpless and stark naked on the floor! I mustn't forget to have a look at your finger before we go to bed.'

They finished the bottle of wine, ate more cheese and talked about what Harry would do while Abigail was at work the next day.

'Study, of course, and there must be something I can do to be useful. You'll be out there earning a living and I'll be here with very little to do. Just tell me, and then you don't have to do housework in the evenings or next weekend, or whenever you usually do it.'

'I can't think of anything in particular,' said Abigail who felt he would be far better employed learning about her world than doing housework. 'You know, I think I'll order a set of those dish drawers we talked about and get this beast out of the house. As I said earlier, I've thought about it, but I never got around to doing it.'

'OK, now it's time to look at that cut,' said Harry as they went upstairs. Your bathroom or mine? Well, I know it's not mine, but I think about it as mine.'

'Of course it's yours. We'd better use mine because that's where the first aid things are.'

Harry studied what was in the first aid drawer and picked out what he thought they needed without hesitation while Abigail watched and wondered how he seemed to know the type of supplies he needed, even though the brand names were probably different from those he was used to.

'How do you know so much about first aid, even wound tape and disinfectants?' she asked and watched his capable hands arrange things in a row beside the basin and thought of how nice it had felt to be touched by him.

'The kind of sites I went to were often remote, so you had to be prepared to look after things yourself – cuts and grazes, thorns deeply embedded. And snake bites too, but that only happened once and I had anti-venom serum, so the guy survived. I don't know how many times I've attended to injured workmen in those places – dozens probably, over the years.' He shook his head at the memories. 'Initial site exploration, drilling core samples and digging out rocks for testing et cetera – lots of mishaps. We had a guy with a badly crushed finger once - a real test of my amateur skills.'

'Ouch,' said Abigail when the three plasters had been pulled off. The finger looked white and compressed, and the deep cut on her fingertip gaped slightly.

'Look at me, not at the finger,' said Harry firmly, and when she still stared at the cut he put two fingers under her chin and turned her face towards him. 'Everything hurts more if you watch, it's a scientific fact, so please do as I say.'

Chuckling inwardly at this display of bossiness, Abigail obeyed and tried to avoid twitching while the cut was cleaned, before he pushed the edges together and secured them tightly, first with first wound tape and then sticking plaster.

'There, and the sticking plaster should make sure it doesn't leak. All done and you didn't look –

very good!' And once again, instead of letting go of her hand, he curled his hand around hers and kissed her fingers then said quickly, 'Sorry! I didn't mean to do that, please forget it!'

'No, I don't want to forget it,' said Abigail calmly. 'I liked it. Nobody's ever done that to me before.' And then, to avoid any further discussion that might reveal too much about how she felt about him, she said quickly. 'And tomorrow I'm picking up my new car at lunchtime, so if you're watching the camera on the app on my laptop, you'll see light coloured Kia EV6 coming up the driveway about half past five or so instead of a black Ford.'

Sitting up in bed Abigail jotted down some notes on the pad she kept on her bedside table and checked the security camera app on her phone. Aaron hadn't been near the house since his surprise visit, but she left the camera to film continually, put the phone down and fell sleep as soon as the turned the light off.

16

The next morning Abigail was up earlier than usual, and when Harry came down she was sitting at the table checking camera footage on the security system. She pointed at the coffee machine where a mug was waiting. "Make yourself a real coffee – I just found the spare packet of coffee capsules, so you don't have to boil the jug. And could you pull down the lever on the toaster too, please. I just checked and Aaron hasn't been back, but there's a couple of precautions I'd like to tell you about.'

He made his coffee, waited for the toaster to do its job and put four slices of toast on a plate. 'Do you really think he'll come back?'

'I don't know, but he started sitting in his car across the road again a few weeks ago. He hadn't done that for a while. I get alerts on my phone when his car is out there, so if I'm out I know not to head home until he's left. His car triggers the camera, but not his face - or not yet.'

The expression she thought of as "question mode" instantly appeared on Harry's face. 'How does that work?'

'The updated security system is very clever, genius really. I uploaded images of his car, front, back and side views, so now I get an alert if his car is within the range of the sensor zone. Which is set very wide and goes right across the street. I've had another few SUVs like his trigger the camera, but I know when it's him, he parks across the street and stares at the house. But if he approached on foot there would be no warning, of course.'

'And what are the precautions? Something I should do while you're at work?'

'I thought we'd have the roller blinds down on this side all the time – both kitchen windows and the window beside the front door, because that's where someone could look in and see you're at home. I bought these blinds after Rob and I discussed stalking, when I was trying to think of ways to avoid hassles. They let in daylight, and you can see out, but you can't see in from the outside – something about the mesh texture, like a one-way mirror. And if the light's on in the kitchen, as it needs to be before I get home from work at this time of the year, you don't turn on the ceiling light, just those three uplighters on the wall. I felt very uncomfortable about Aaron sitting out there watching me move around inside the house, so I always pull the blind down after dark, but now I think we'll leave them down all the time.'

He looked slightly stunned. 'Do we need to check he can't see in with the kitchen wall lights on?'

'I've done that. He knows now that you're staying here, but if he can see you're at home in the daytime when I'm at work, he might try to get you to admit him, to open the door if he knocks. And he always knocks, he never uses the doorbell. I saw you trying out the peephole in the front door yesterday, so there's another thing to keep us from having to talk to him again.'

Harry nodded and gazed at the kitchen window where the nearly invisible blind was pulled right down. 'I noticed those blinds yesterday – incredible how you hardly see them in daylight, very clever.'

Abigail pushed the butter towards him when his hand reached for another slice of toast. 'And I'd rather he couldn't tell if I'm here or not, or even where I am in the house. I often leave lights on when I go out at night, so he probably knows that means nothing. I know I sound paranoid, but being pursued and watched is unnerving.'

'You're such an asset as a guest,' she said when she got home that night and found Harry cooking. 'I've never had anyone but me cook a meal in this kitchen. Thank you!'

'No need to thank me – I enjoy cooking. How is

your finger today? Is it sore from using it on the keyboard? I suppose you use a computer a lot at work.'

'I've already learnt to use my middle finger instead, but it feels a lot better already. Is that the dryer I can hear?'

'I put a load in the washing machine and now it's drying … I hope. I had to look things up online because I've never used a dryer before, but it seems to be working ok.' He grinned. 'I didn't want to risk putting something in that would melt or shrink or whatever if I set it to what the machine vaguely calls "hot". I mean, how hot its hot?'

It made her laugh, all this domestic activity and coming home to a house where there was nothing much that needed doing. The change from her lonely existence since Mike's death was nearly overwhelming. 'You'd better watch it,' she said. 'I could get used to this, such a treat!'

He gave her one of those looks she was getting familiar with. 'Ha! Says the domestic goddess, who doesn't need any help, really. But as I said before, I should make myself useful. Did you pick up the new car?'

She couldn't believe she hadn't told him straight off. 'Yes! Come and have a look!'

The new car, shiny ice-blue with lines that made it look as if it had been origami-folded and then unfolded, looked immense compared to Abigial's old car.

'Huge!' Harry walked around it, looking closely from all angles. 'Kia EV6, what does EV stand for?'

'Electric Vehicle, just the common abbreviation. I'm having a so called wall-box installed next week – so I can fast-charge it right here.'

Harry paused in his second circuit around the car and looked at her across the roof. 'Aren't all cars electric?'

'God, no! Electric cars are still a minority, but when Mike died, and I sold his SUV I decided that once I'd done some research I would by an electric.'

They were having dinner when Abigail thought of something. 'Listen, I had an idea today. I'll get a cell phone for you and then you can message me if you want me to pick something up in town or whatever.'

'No, please don't!' His reaction was instant and his expression serious. 'You're doing too much for me already. Buying stuff for me is taking it too far.'

To avoid him feeling guilty about it she said, trying to sound casually light-hearted, 'Don't be an idiot, Harry! This is like an adventure, it's interesting and challenging and kind of fun – and totally incredible, of course. Let's not forget incredible. And remember all that money? Let's put it to good use. Exactly the sort of crazy thing Mike would approve of for me to do with those millions.'

'Really? You think he'd approve of all this? Me living here, and you doing all these things for me?'

'He definitely would,' said Abigail. 'He'd be so pleased I had company, and he'd like you, he really would. You're just the type of guy he liked, someone who knew a lot of things he didn't, science type things. So that story we told Aaron couldn't have been more apt, and in another timestream it might have happened exactly as we said.'

After dinner Abigail pulled the curtains across the big living room windows that overlooked the back garden and they watched a re-run of the TV news, so Harry could come to grips with current affairs as they happened.

'That was today's update for you! Let's have a Baileys.' She turned the TV off and headed for the sideboard. 'I haven't had one for ages. One of those little habits that drop by the wayside when you suddenly find yourself living on you own.'

Harry looked thoughtfully at the little glass with milky looking then smelt it. 'What is this? It smells delicious, I've never heard of this before.' Then he tasted it and grinned. 'Very nice!'

Abigail knew what she would do next and smiled at the thought of how much he would like another taste discovery. 'But now, tell me about cars in your timestream. Are all your vehicles electric?'

'I think the last ones that ran on oil based fuel were outlawed in most countries in the 1970's or thereabouts, maybe a bit later. Lots of people have kept them as curiosities and the car museum downtown has a few iconic ones. I went for a drive in a diesel fuelled truck a couple of years ago in Afghanistan - very noisy!'

'So in your world they must have been working

on developing good batteries much earlier than we did here. Interesting! What kind are they?'

'Lithium anode batteries are the most common, but some cars have graphene batteries. My car was a Ford Stealth with a lithium anode battery – huge capacity, very effective and capable of being recharged to a hundred percent nearly indefinitely.'

'You'll have to search the internet and check if we have those, I wouldn't have a clue. I just watched YouTube videos about electric cars until I found one that got good reviews and had good safety ratings. I don't know what kind of battery the Kia has. Wait here and I'll bring something else for you to try.'

Returning with two bowls Abigail stopped by the sideboard, poured Bailey's over the vanilla ice cream and handed one to Harry. 'Try this!

'The best new taste yet! Let's have this every night – and when I earn money again I'll buy all the supplies.'

They smiled at each other and ate their ice cream in companiable silence.

17

*A*bigail was still caught in her nightmare and struggled to understand if the voice repeatedly saying her name was part of the dream or not.

'Abigail, please wake up!' The voice was insistent. 'You're having a bad dream, you're crying.'

She opened her eyes and saw Harry kneeling beside her bed in the dark. Crying? She touched her wet face and sat up, feeling dislocated and muddled. 'I had a nightmare,' she said, her voice thick with tears and wiped her wet cheeks with her hands. 'It's one I have now and then, and I can't ...' Her voice broke on a sob, she covered her face with both hands unable to continue.

'Do you want to tell me?' asked Harry quietly. 'Would it make it go away? Make it less real?'

She didn't know what to say. The recurring nightmare was sometimes so real while it played out in her sleeping mind that when she woke up she couldn't tell where she was – back in that awful past or safely here and now. Her let hands drop and sighed. 'But it *is* real. Or it was. It's something that happened a long time ago and I have this dream every so often, still, after all this time.'

'Tell me about it,' he urged gently. 'What happened? Something so bad it's still with you. If we talk about it you might get some relief.'

'I've never talked about it with anyone since the day it happened. I only told the girl who was my flatmate back then, and I didn't tell her any details.' She wasn't sure why she was telling him this. After keeping it to herself for so long, never explaining her occasional nightmares to Mike and never confiding in anyone, apart from that sketchy version she told Lou, suddenly the temptation to tell someone what had really happened was overwhelming.

'I had a boyfriend, a man much older than myself when I was twenty.' She hesitated only for a moment. 'He used to hurt me.'

'How did he hurt you?' Harry's voice was still quiet but there was a tension behind the words that he couldn't hide. 'What did he do?'

'Three times he grabbed me by the throat and choked me when he lost his temper and ...' She stopped when she realised her hands had gone to her neck as if to protect herself.

'And?'

'The last time he did it, I passed out. I came to lying on the sofa in his living room and he was watching TV. We'd been sitting there watching the tennis, and we had an argument about something minor, and he lost his temper – again.'

She paused again, not sure if he wanted to hear the whole sad story or if this was enough. 'And then? Did you leave him?'

'I wasn't living with him,' she said and for some reason continued with what happened next, which still had the power to make her feel sick, 'I got up to go to the bathroom, I felt dizzy and weird, unbalanced - and he said quite casually, "If you're making coffee, could you make me one too?" as if nothing had happened. I looked at myself in the mirror in the hall and I had bruises forming already, dark finger marks, and my neck hurt when I touched them. Really hurt, as if something was damaged deep inside.'

Now she felt as if she was back there, and that quiet determination she had so surprisingly dredged up that ghastly day still surprised her. 'I just picked up my jacket, which was on a chair in the hall and walked out the door. I never talked to him again.'

'Did he try?'

'Oh yes, he tried several times. Once he stood outside my flat for a couple of hours waiting for me to come out. My flatmate saw him when she came home from work, and she kept an eye on him through the window. I'd told her that he'd hurt me badly and that he scared me, and that I didn't want to see him. So, she went outside and told him she'd just called the cops, and they were on their way, and she was going to report him for assault.'

Abigail nearly smiled in the dark at the memory of her staunch flatmate. 'When she came upstairs again and told me what she'd done I couldn't believe it, but it worked – I never set eyes on him again.' After a moment she added, 'Apart from in these nightmares. Being strangled is really terrifying, Harry, it's hard to describe what it's like, and that's what I re-live in my nightmares. The panic of being unable to breathe and then your vision goes blurry and there's this loud buzzing sound in your ears …'

'But later, when you met Mike – didn't he do anything about it?'

'I never told him.'

'What?!' Harry's voice rose in surprise, and she knew that now she had to tell him the rest.

'I met Mike only a month or so later, through friends we had in common, but I knew if I told him he'd go after this guy, and it would end up in court, and at the time I just couldn't deal with it. I still had nightmares about it all the time, about being choked to death, and I thought if I had to be interviewed and be a witness or whatever, I might crack, so I said nothing.' She paused, thought of her hesitation back then and how she had eventually known she must do something to protect others. 'And then after a while I realised I must, in case he did it to someone else, and I googled his name to see if he'd been accused of anything like it before – and he was dead! He died in a three-car crash on the motorway just a few weeks after the day when I walked out of his house. So there was no point.'

She stopped talking, slid down in the bed and lay on her side facing him with an agonising cramp at the back of her neck. She rubbed it hard with her fingers while she waited to hear what he would say.

'You said that you never told anyone apart from a short version you told your flatmate? But when you had these terrible nightmares, didn't Mike ask what you dreamt about?'

'I didn't tell him, I just said it was something horrible, but I couldn't remember the details.'

'Why didn't you tell him?'

'I don't know. I had a feeling he might not have been able to deal with it. You know, something emotional and intangible like that. He was a very practical man, he liked to think he could step in and fix things in a practical way, if you know what I mean or remove irritating obstacles from my life, and he was very protective, so if he couldn't make the nightmares go away he would have felt he'd failed.' She sighed at the memory. 'I just let him think I was prone to nightmares. ' She rubbed the back or her neck again and tried to reach lower down. 'You should go back to bed. I'm so sorry I woke you up.'

It was only later that she realised that by telling Harry about an event she had not been able to share with Mike, she had told him how much she trusted him. And not only that, but that she already understood his personality and how empathetic he was.

Without replying Harry reached over her and gripped her shoulders with strong, warm hands. Slowly and carefully he turned her over until she was lying on her front, and she didn't make a move to resist. The re-lived trauma had exhausted her, and she knew Harry wouldn't hurt her. Then she felt his hands on her back, firm fingers probing both sides of her spine between her shoulder blades and she let out a quiet, 'Ouch!'

'That's the spot,' he said, and his fingers probed and rubbed for a few minutes until suddenly the muscle spasm let go and the pain was gone. Abigail sighed with relief. 'Thank you – that's wonderful!'

'Stay like that,' he said when she made a move to turn over, so she did, caught in the spell of a moment that felt like magic, content to let him do whatever he wanted. His hands worked up and down her back, gently and slowly, and with no transition from being awake to falling asleep, she was deeply and dreamlessly asleep.

When her phone alarm went off in the morning Abigail woke up with a feeling of such deep relief that for a moment it confused her, and then she remembered what had happened in the night. She wondered what it would be like when she and Harry met this morning, if she would feel embarrassed about having told him and the way he manhandled her to fix her aching neck. Would he refer to it? And if he did, how would she respond? But no answers were forthcoming, of course, because this was a new and untested situation. She went to have a shower and stood dreamily letting the hot water run down her back, still undecided about what to say when she went downstairs.

Harry was already sitting at the kitchen table reading something on the laptop with his customary look of intense concentration. He looked up, smiled and went back to his reading, and Abigail made a detour around the table, picked up his empty coffee mug and briefly touched shoulder. 'Thank you!'

When she put a fresh mug of coffee beside him he looked up. 'Are you OK?'

'I'm fine, thanks to you – I feel great.' And nothing more was said.

18

_A_fter a stressful day when more than one thing had gone wrong Abigail arrived home later than usual. She had been the last person to leave her section of the Court House, and to top it off she got soaked on her way to the car.

'Hi,' she said, when she had hung her wet coat in the garage and came through the connecting door to the kitchen and saw Harry doing something at the stove. 'What are you up to?'

'Making dinner,' he said, as if this was perfectly normal. 'You look as if you got caught in the rain.'

'I had a shitty day – a meeting that was meant to take an hour max took nearly two because two guys kept arguing over a meaningless point, and then I had to finish a couple of urgent things, so I was late leaving. And as a nice end to the day, the door that leads nearly straight to the carpark was locked, and I couldn't open it, so I had to go back through to the staff entrance on the far side of the building and walk around. And it was pouring – freezing rain blowing sideways, very close to turning into snow, I think.'

This litany of misery didn't make Harry either exclaim in sympathy or look dismissive, he just said calmly, 'Why don't you have a hot shower and get out of those damp clothes? The dinner can wait, it's not a culinary masterpiece and it won't spoil. Take your time – you clearly need to relax and slow down a bit.'

She smiled at how domestic this seemed and went gratefully upstairs and decided a long, hot shower would be the perfect thing before dinner. Fifteen minutes later, when she came through the door from the bathroom to her bedroom, she heard Astrid's voice downstairs calling out a cheerful, 'Hellooo!'

Oh, no! This wasn't supposed to happen! Now she must quickly throw on some clothes and go downstairs, where Astrid would now have come across Harry. After scrambling into a sweatshirt and a pair of trackpants in record time, she ran downstairs on bare feet and found Astrid and Harry in the kitchen silently looking at each other. But what had he said when Astrid asked who he was, as she would surely have done? They turned slightly tense faces towards her, as if they expected her to resolve this impasse, but how could she when she had no idea what he had said?

'Hi,' she said and tried to decide how to proceed. 'Have you two introduced yourselves?'

Astrid gave her an incredulous look and said in a disbelieving voice, 'I just let myself in with my key because I saw your bedroom and bathroom lights on, and I thought you might be having a bath or something. And when I asked this guy who he is, he just said he's Harry … and then you came down. So no, we haven't really been introduced.'

Harry's face was calm, but she could sense his tension like a swirl of turbulent air. He was leaving it to her to decide what she wanted Astrid to know, and all she could think was that she wished they had planned for this and agreed on tactics. But common sense snapped into place and she decided to let Astrid in on the story. It would be much better to tell her the truth now rather than later, when she would feel as if Abigail hadn't trusted her.

'Harry dropped in unexpectedly,' she said, trying to sound casual, and nearly giggled at what an apt description that was. 'He's staying for a few days. Let's sit down and have a wine or something, so you can get to know him. Would you like to stay for dinner?'

Astrid looked from Abigail to Harry and back again with an expression of total outrage. 'He was *cooking*!' she said in an accusing tone of voice. 'He's making dinner in *your* kitchen! And I've never even *heard* of him.'

'Wine, and beer for you, so you can drive home later, and then we'll sit down with some chips and dip and tell you who Harry is, and why he's here.' She smiled at Harry and added casually, 'Provided you don't mind, of course.'

'It's up to you. It's probably best that she knows, I suppose, and we can re-heat the dinner later. I'll get the snacks if you get the drinks.'

Astrid's eyes swung back to Abigail's face at this demonstration of casual familiarity, and her expression said everything: outrage and suspicion.

'Do sit down, darling,' said Abigail to her glaring baby sister and gave her a little push. 'You'll get the full story in a minute, but first I want to show you something on my laptop.'

She pulled the laptop over and sat down next to Astrid and opened the clip of Harry's arrival, which she had saved as a separate file. 'And don't frown like that, everything is fine, just watch this and tell me what you think.'

She and Harry kept their eyes on Astrid's face as she watched the short video, but apart from a gasp or two there was no comment when she reached the end, she just played it from the beginning again, and then a third time with intense concentration, leaning close to the screen and hardly blinking. Finally she looked up and exclaimed loudly, startling them both, 'Oh my God! I don't believe it! It's The Time Traveller's Wife - *exactly* the same! And you're called *Harry* – even better!'

She burst out laughing and couldn't stop, and laughed on and on, nearly out of control. They watched in disbelieving silence and waited for this hysterical outburst to stop, until she gradually calmed down and wiped tears from her cheeks. 'You know, that book they made into a film! Haven't you read it? You *must* have read it!'

Abigail shook her head. 'I know the name, but I haven't read it. Do explain because we're both baffled. I thought you'd be really surprised by that video clip, or maybe refuse to believe it, but it seems to be more like a comedy skit suddenly. Why is this funny?'

'Drinks first,' said Harry and put glasses on the table. 'Let's get comfortable before we start.' He grinned at Astrid. 'Not that I have the faintest idea what that book is about, but I'm glad you find it amusing and stopped looking at me as if I'm a dangerous criminal.'

Astrid opened the can of beer, filled her glass and took a big gulp before she replied. 'That book is about a guy called Henry – get it? Henry and Harry, isn't it great? And he travels back and forth between time periods, so sometimes he's talking to his future wife when she's a little kid, and sometimes he's way ahead, so knows what will happen much further on, before the period they really live in. He has no control over it, it just happens.' She held her glass up in a toast. 'And Henry *always* arrives in a different time zone, if we can call it that, naked and with no belongings, leaving his clothes and empty shoes behind wherever he was when time snatched him away without warning. So what era are you from?'

Before Harry could reply, Abigail asked, 'So you believe what you saw in the video?'

'Well, I've got to, don't I?' said Astrid without hesitation, as if what Abigail had asked was ridiculous. 'It's totally crazy, and it can't really have happened, but it *did*. The last time I watched it I went super slow and kept my eyes on the time stamp and there's not a single second missing, so it's obviously true. And no footprints to where he appeared in the middle of the lawn, and he didn't fall from the sky – he's just suddenly there. *Epic!*'

'I'm from 2029,' said Harry cautiously, 'but not the 2029 you'll be living in a few years from now. I was in a different branch of time, which Abigail and I call a timestream. There's a lot of stuff we don't know, and we'll never find out, but my timestream must have split off from this one quite a long time ago, ,we're not quite sure when, but in this timestream my father didn't marry my mother, he married a woman I've never heard of. So here he's not my father. Nobody is, I never existed here.'

'Wow, epic!' exclaimed Astrid again and took another big swallow of her beer. 'Hang on, let me think – do you exist in two places now? Or did you disappear from the era you came from? And do you think you'll go back?'

Harry glanced at Abigail and shook his head. 'Too many questions and we have no answers,' said Abigail. 'Basically, we don't know any more than you do, we've just had a bit longer to get used to it. But for the moment Harry's living in the guest room, he's taken over Mike's clothes, the ones people won't recognise as Mike's, and he's staying inside until Jasper comes next week.'

'OK, that makes sense,' said Astrid slowly. 'For now, anyway. But I've got a lot of extra questions, so do you mind if I ask? I kind of feel I'm suspended midair, and I don't know how to get down.'

'She always had a way with words,' said Abigail in a pretend aside to Harry.' Right from when she was tiny she used language like artists use paints – very expressive.'

'Of course you can ask.' Harry pulled the bowl of chips over to his side of the table, out of Astrid's reach and grinned at her expression of surprise. 'We'll eat these as a favour to you while we listen to your list of questions, so you don't have to talk with your mouth full.'

He likes her, thought Abigail, and he knows just how to handle her to avoid those sometimes difficult moments when she imagines people are being patronising or dismissive. What a great talent for someone who never had a child of his own.

'Right, so off the top of my head, number one is this, how did it happen? And number two, who is Jasper? And number three, what if Aaron comes calling again? And number four, how will Harry function here if he never existed, which I suppose he doesn't – or didn't, until now? And ...'

'Stop!' said Abigail and held her hand up, palm out like someone directing traffic. 'That's enough for now. For a start, Jasper is a guy I used to work with in Wellington, an IT security specialist of a very specialised kind, who owes me a huge favour. He's coming down for a couple of days next week when I'm on leave, and he'll hopefully find a way to create a background for Harry.'

'Did you work together in that secret place you refuse to tell me about? Neat! Will I get to meet him?'

'You can come and meet him, but don't expect someone who looks like some movie spy or something. I know what your imagination is like! He's a great, burly guy with a shock of curly hair – or at least he still had a lot of hair last time I saw him a couple of years ago. But he's totally reliable and I would trust him with my life. Every year, on the anniversary of the day I saved his career a dozen years ago, he sends me a message that says he owes me and to let him know any time I need help. Which I've just done.'

'Cool! And Aaron? Can you fudge it if he sees Harry? I know he's come here uninvited before, after Mike died.'

'He already did, a couple of days ago. Harry was upstairs and came down just in time to interrupt Aaron trying to be a bit hands-on.'

They told her what had happened, how Harry had listened from halfway down the stairs and decided to intervene. 'Fabulous performance,' said Abigail with a fond glance at Harry, and thought, I bet he's wondering if I'm going to mention the knuckle kiss! 'Between us we acted out a really convincing story of how we've known each other for years after meeting on a holiday and all going skiing together. And now I think of it, we must tell Jasper all that too, so it can become part of what he can construct as a life story for Harry. How about dinner now?'

19

The bustle of setting the table and Harry getting dinner going again turned out to be a perfect interlude of normality and also, thought Abigail, the perfect situation for Astrid to gradually understand how laid-back and nice Harry was. Not that she wouldn't discover it in time, or perhaps she already had, but to see him quietly doing his thing and not attempting to be part of the casual talk between her and Astrid was the perfect demonstration.

The meal turned into exactly what Abigail had expected; more questions from Astrid and explanations, as far as possible, from her and Harry, and surprisingly, a lot of laughter.

'You must miss your wife, and you don't know if you'll ever get back to her! So sad! Do you have children?' asked Astrid without a thought of discretion or embarrassment.

Abigail saw the slight hesitation on Harry's face

as he tried to decide how to reply, and she was certain there was trauma behind the way he never mentioned her. So she stepped in to reduce the risk of Astrid asking too many follow-on questions, if he told her he had a wife.

'Luckily no complications of that kind at all,' she intervened before Harry got his answer sorted out. 'He's not married and no children - imagine how awful that would be! But extended family and friends – that's a huge loss. Imagine if you got whisked off to some other timestream and never knew if you'd get back. You'd miss me, wouldn't you?'

Astrid looked so guilt stricken that Abigail had to hide a smile. 'I'm sorry, Harry, I just didn't think! I got carried away by the whole thing, it's so incredible, but of course you must feel devasted by what you've lost, parents and family. What was your job? I mean, what is your job?'

And from there the discussion turned more to what they imagined Jasper might be able to create in the way of background, and if Harry would be able to work as a geologist or have to think of another career.

'But listen! You could do anything,' said Astrid enthusiastically. 'Think of all the people who wish they weren't tied down to commitments of various kinds, like mortgages and bad marriages or having to look after elderly parents. They can't just say, oh, I think I'll give up my well paid job as a geologist and start a gardening service or maybe become a kayaking guide or something. They're locked in.'

'Later on, after Jasper's been and we know a bit more, we'll sit down and tell you what I've already told Abigail about my timestream,' said Harry seriously and Astrid sat up straighter at the tone of his voice. 'You wouldn't enjoy the world I came from, not at all. I imagine you would call it dystopian and totalitarian. So if I seem surprisingly calm and happy it's because this place is like heaven to me, like a revelation.'

'Wow! Can you tell me now? Please?'

'No, not tonight,' said Harry firmly. 'It will take time, particularly seeing how fast you think up more questions, so we'll leave it for now, but we'll do it later - I promise. And now you must promise me something in return. Something very important.'

Her eyes widened at his tone of voice, and she raised her chin. 'I'll promise anything! You've trusted me with some stuff I'm sure you'd rather not have told me, so I'll promise whatever you want.'

'Not one single word of this can go outside this house – nothing! If it stays between the four of us – that's including Jasper – I'm safe. If any of it is even hinted at I might face consequences I can't even imagine. Perhaps even mental hospital, certainly nothing even remotely like what Abigail is setting up for me. And the publicity would be rampant, I imagine – people speculating that I'm a fraud and just after attention or something.'

'Done!' said Astrid and got up, walked around the table and held her hand out. 'I promise.'

When Astrid left just after eleven, Harry looked at Abigail and uttered a heartfelt, 'Wow!' Abigail had to laugh. 'Is that a new word for you? Astrid says it all the time, and yes, that went well. And you were so patient when she started asking things, far more than most people would be.'

He smiled. 'I enjoyed her. She's very direct and also very endearing - the enthusiasm! You're lucky to have such a great little sister.'

'I know. We have our little problems, like her complete inability to stick to a budget and not overspend, and a few other minor things. I'm a dozen years older and she listens to me, which she might not if we were closer in age.'

She tied up the rubbish bag and went to put it in the trundler in the garage and when she came back, Harry had put the last dishes in the dishwasher and was drying his hands.

'Now tell me, what was that funny look about when we told her about me interrupting Aaron's advances?'

'I don't know what you mean,' said Abigail and tried to think of something to explain it, something that wouldn't make her blush, and she certainly wasn't about to mention the knuckle kiss. 'I can't remember a funny look.'

'Liar,' he said gently and ran one fingertip slowly down her cheek. 'You're blushing. I think I can guess. Don't worry, there's no hurry.'

And on that cryptic note they turned the lights off and went upstairs, where Abigail lay awake for a long time trying to decide if her first reaction to that last comment of his was right, before she finally fell asleep long after midnight.

When Abigail came home from work on Wednesday evening with the pizza she had promised, Harry was just plugging in Mike's laptop to charge at the far end of the kitchen bench.

'Let me take that,' he said and put the box on the table, and Abigail shrugged her jacket off and went to hang it up before she poured them both a glass of wine.

'Oh, I nearly forgot!' She went back to the garage and returned with a little bag. 'Here's your phone. The same as mine but with a blue cover so we can tell them apart. I've loaded my number on it and Astrid's, so you have two people you can text or call. I'll show you were to find the apps later.'

'Thank you! I'll learn all about it tomorrow morning. I looked for Barton Wilder today,' said Harry when Abigail put the glass in front of him. He moved her laptop to the far end of the table and stacked his notes into a tidy pile. 'I went on … what's it called … Facebook, on your laptop, but I didn't find him, so I searched the whole internet and there are some Barton Wilders in the US, but not a single one in this country.'

'Who's Barton Wilder? You haven't mentioned him before.' Abigail watched the expression on Henrey's face change and wondered if he wished he hadn't mentioned this person, who obviously brought back bad memories. 'Is he a friend of yours?'

'No … he's Katrina 's lover. I only just found out about it a couple of days before I left for Brazil, it was quite new. A bit of a shock, and I hadn't done anything about it yet.'

'Oh my God, you poor man! How did you find out?'

Clearing his throat, he looked slightly to one side of her, as if not seeing her expression would make it easier to tell her.

'I'd been in Wellington in a meeting with some government officials about exploration in the Southern Basin, and I managed to catch an earlier flight back. I'd forgotten that Katrina had the day off as compensation for doing an extra night shift, so I didn't call her. I just thought I'd be there at the end of the day when she came home, like a nice surprise.' He shook his head. 'The irony of it! I let myself in and looking down the hallway I saw her sitting in a chair in the living room, kind of side-on to me. She was painting her toenails, and the phone was on the armrest of her chair, on speaker. She was talking to her best friend, Jenny, who lives in Auckland.'

He stopped talking for a moment, lost in the memory and Abigail waited patiently. 'We'd only been married for a year. We met at a wedding and got married six months later.'

'And you heard something that upset you, I can see it on your face.'

Maybe she shouldn't ask direct questions, but he had just told her he had researched his wife's lover. It might be insensitive, and it was strictly speaking not her business to probe, but she knew she would only be able to help him construct a life in this timestream if she knew the obstacles they might come up against. She had wondered about his wife after seeing his reaction when Astrid asked if he was married, not to mention that he'd not included her, when he listed the people who were lost to him, and now he'd just told her his wife had a lover. He needed her. If she handed him over to somebody else, they would never do such a good job as she felt sure she could do, not to mention the advantage of having Jasper on hand and all that he might be able to achieve. She had to know more.

'So, what did Katrina say to her friend?'

'It was obviously a recap on how she and I had met and got married so quickly,' he said quietly. 'Jenny was still living in France when we got married, she had only returned to New Zealand at the end of the summer, and maybe they were just catching up on the details of how it all happened. Katrina had just got to the point in the story when she discovered after our first date what my net worth is. No sorry, that should be what my net worth *was* - and that I'd inherited a lot of money from my father. She was telling Jenny how she had started a quest to find out from others what I liked, every aspect of my preferences from books and films to food.' He gave Abigail a wry smile, and she could think of nothing to say.

'I stood in the hallway frozen to the spot. There was absolutely no doubt it was the truth - she was enjoying being able to tell someone how clever she'd been. At one stage she laughed and said that though she didn't like Japanese food and would rather have fried chicken, she pretended sushi was a favourite of hers because it was another detail to make the bond stronger. She'd made a list, would you believe.'

His voice wasn't bitter, but she sensed that telling her about this was hard work, probably because of how he felt; that he had been fooled and humiliated. She had a feeling that behind his quiet façade he was furious with himself for falling for such an elaborate scam.

'They were laughing about it and because the phone was on speaker I could hear Jenny's responses and her questions, so I could tell that she had heard about this before but not in such detail.'

Harry's eyes drifted away from her for a moment, and she waited quietly until she felt sufficient time had passed, that she wasn't interrupting some thought process or pressuring him too hard. 'What did you do?'

'I know it seems strange, but as I stood there in the hall hearing this I felt there was only one thing I could do. I had to remove myself to avoid an out of control situation, to think about what I should do.' Abigail nodded. 'I walked out the door, which I hadn't yet closed behind me, and went for a five minute walk, then I returned and made it obvious I was home. It feels so strange now I'm in this timestream, like I'm furious about something that never happened.'

'And sad, I presume?'

'Sad? No, I'm not sad. I had wondered for some time what was wrong with our relationship, why I felt as if we had nothing in common despite all the things we *did* have in common. But of course, we didn't have anything in common - that was just Katrina's carefully constructed fiction.'

Harry picked up his glass and rotated it slowly between his fingers, and then suddenly he started talking very fast, as if he was suddenly desperate to tell someone every single detail of that overhead conversation.

'The woman I married wasn't a real person. She was assembled from carefully selected parts to make a composite woman who'd be perfect for me. I mean, take someone who's smart and sexy and has a wonderful figure and a great smile, then add a layer of pretend preferences and interests to match your own. It was irresistible, I couldn't believe I'd found someone with so many qualities I liked, a perfect match as they say. At one point she told Jenny that it had been like creating a figure of Lego blocks. Put a pink piece here because it's pretty, put a red block there to indicate she's passionate and add a dark blue for seriousness - then stand the thing on its little block feet and Snap! there you have her, the perfect match for Harry.'

Abigail considered for a moment then shook her head. 'But it doesn't make sense! If Katrina spent so much time and effort hooking you in and making sure she'd have access to your money, why did she start an affair and risk it all? It seems like she was doing something counter to her own best interests.'

'I don't know, but I guess it's in her nature to always want what's new and shiny, something desirable, and in this case that was the man she was having an affair with – Barton Wilder.'

He drank some wine and gave Abigail a little smile. 'Don't look like that. I'm not going to break down and cry. In a strange way I feel that I'm talking about somebody else – that what I've just told you is a story I read in a book. Even though it's only a few weeks ago, or at least in my mind it's a few weeks, the situation seems unreal now and without substance. But I'm furious with myself for allowing her to manipulate me so easily.'

'It must have been hard,' said Abigail after a moment's consideration, as she played out the scene he had described in her mind. 'I can't imagine discovering something like that and not mentioning it for several days and then going away on an overseas trip and leaving it unresolved.'

He sighed. 'I know. Maybe it makes me sound hard, but first I had to figure out exactly what I was going to do about it, find the right words to discuss what I'd overheard and tell her I was divorcing her. And remember that to start with I didn't know about the affair, that wasn't part of the conversation I overheard. But a couple of days later, when I was about to face her before I left for Brazil, a colleague took me aside and said his wife knew that Katrina was having a torrid affair with a surgeon. So, I postponed my talk with Katrina, I just couldn't face it right then and decided to do it as soon as I got home from Brazil. In the meantime I'd do some research and email my lawyer to check the legal options regarding my assets.'

Without looking at him while she topped up their glasses Abigail asked quietly, 'Did it wipe out the feelings you had for her when your friend told you about the lover? Or had you already managed to distance yourself emotionally when you found out how she had scammed you?'

Harry held up his glass and studied the colour of the wine. 'This wine is such a dark red, it's nearly black - and that hint of black currant. It must be a Syrah.'

It made Abigail smile to hear him casually change the subject and comment on the wine, such a normal and laid back thing to do in the middle of telling a tragic personal story. 'It's an Australian Syrah, one of my favourites.'

'But you're completely right.' Harry held up his glass in a mock toast. 'I think hearing that vivid description of how she constructed a persona to scam me, as if she was building a figure out of Lego bricks, and how she laughed about her clever deceit– it removed the emotional connection, chopped through it like a knife. And then finding out that she was having an affair, that was the final insult. There was no affection left.'

'I can't get over it,' said Abigail slowly, trying to find the right words.' I simply can't imagine how you did it. Stayed in the same house for another couple of days, then found out people knew she was having an affair and then left for the other side of the world. Weren't you itching to have it out with her right there and then? Or couldn't you be bothered right then?'

'Exactly! And as I said, I wanted to find out the legal situation before I acted. There was a lot of family money involved, and I didn't feel she deserved to share it. In my timestream my dad wasn't a schoolteacher, he was an industrialist on quite a large scale.' He gave her a wry smile. 'And now, unless I somehow get moved back there, I'll never know how it turned out. I've presumably returned from Brazil and confronted Katrina in that other timestream. So, now I've got to push it to one side and regard it as something I read about, not something that was part of my life, or I'll be furious forever.'

'But at the start you loved her?'

'I thought I did, and isn't it odd that I loved someone who was full of deceit and pretence, only after what my money could provide? That not the slightest hint of her real character came through to warn me about what she was really like.' And then to her surprise he laughed, a genuine laugh of amusement and said, 'But I'd love to know that I did have it out with her in that other existence, that I told her what I thought about her tactics and ordered her out of the house. Out of this house.'

She couldn't help it; she had to laugh too. 'Just imagine how satisfying that would have been, picture the scene in your mind and it might over-write the anger you feel.'

She noticed his look at the now nearly empty pizza boxes. 'I can't believe we managed to eat a giant pizza without even noticing while you told me about Katrina. You can have that last piece – I've eaten more than my share and I'm full.'

21

The first message from Abigail to Harry's phone was sent when she arrived in the office on Friday morning after she had an idea on the way to work. Best to warn him not to start making dinner, she thought, and texted: *I'm bringing something for dinner again, something you might like.*

He replied ten minutes later, *'Great – thank you!'*

Later that morning Abigail was having a coffee at her desk and Jane joined her, wheeling her desk chair across the big open office as she sometimes did.

'Did Fred ask you out?' she said after carefully checking who was within earshot. 'You know that day when he tried to chat you up – did you go out with him?'

'No way! That's not going to happen – never ever.' Abigail opened her desk drawer and reached for the packet of gingernut biscuits she had won in their weekly Quiz competition. 'Have one of these. How's the great man hunt going? Maybe *you* should go out with Fred.'

'Thank you so much!' said Jane sarcastically. 'But as someone said just recently, that's not going to happen, never ever.'

When Jane got up to return to her desk ten minutes later, Abigail thought of something. 'But why did you ask about Fred just now? He only asked me that one time a few weeks ago.'

'Oh, I just wondered if anything had developed, or if he'd tried again. I heard him on the phone in the lunchroom last week. He didn't know I was just coming along, and I stopped before I got to the door, so I could listen. He was telling someone he would try again, and I knew it was about you because he mentioned "the adorable Abigail". Isn't that sweet? So I thought he might have asked you out again.'

'Yuck!' said Abigail and made a disgusted face. 'I feel sick now – would you pass me the wastepaper basket, please, in case I vomit?'

Jane giggled and wheeled her chair away, and Abigail thought she knew whom Fred had been talking to in that phone call.

'Look what I got, seeing we can't go out and have dinner at a Japanese restaurant. My favourite food –

salmon onigiri and lots of other lovely Japanese things, plus seaweed salad. I remember you said you like Japanese food,' said Abigail that night and put the bag full of take-out boxes on the bench. Behind her, Harry said, 'Are you making a little Lego woman for me now?'

Abigail reacted as if something had struck her from behind and felt a vivid blush erupt on her face. She blinked hard, her hands stopped moving and she just stood there looking down at the food bag unable to move or speak.

'Shit, I'm sorry! That was just a bad joke – please forget I said that.' She must stay facing away from him. If she turned around she would reveal how she felt, she simply couldn't do it. 'Of course,' she said in a tight voice, very unlike her own. 'It doesn't matter.'

Strong hands grasped her upper arms and forced her to face him. 'Yes!' he said. 'It does matter. Come here!'

He pulled her in and held her tight against him with his hands flat on her back, and she felt his warm breath on the side of her head. Time seemed to stop, the world disappeared and all she could feel was his heart beating and his breath on her temple.

'Please, darling – don't take it to heart,' he said quietly. 'It was a stupid quip. I didn't mean it.'

She could hear how much he wanted to comfort her. She sighed and relaxed against him, and one of his hands ran up through her hair and curved around the back of her skull to secure her more firmly against him. After what seemed like an eternity, but was probably only a minute or two, she spoke into his shoulder. 'It's OK now – don't worry, I'm fine, I know you didn't mean it.'

He kissed her temple and let her go, and when he stepped back she felt as if she had woken up from a deep sleep. She gave him a little smile. 'I'm sorry - I overreacted. I know you didn't mean it that way. It was just for a split second and I'm fine. Are you?'

'If you're OK, so am I. Show me what you've got in that bag. Did you get lots of pickled ginger and wasabi?'

'Of course, heaps of pickled ginger, and we have wasabi in the fridge, a nearly new tube. I need a glass of wine. What should we drink with Japanese food? I don't have any rice wine.'

'Oh look, you got yakitori skewers, I love those. Chardonnay would work, I think. Is there any?'

'God yes, go and look in that tall white cabinet in the garage, in the far corner – Mike's ever-growing collection of wine. I haven't bought a bottle of wine since he died, and that cupboard is still nearly full – I hardly ever drink when I'm on my own. Put it in the freezer to cool if it isn't chilled enough from being in the garage. I'll just go up and change.'

I need a few minutes to process this little drama, she thought, as she ran up the stairs. Was that darling phrase the kind of darling expression you use when someone's hurt, a good friend perhaps, or a child, or did he mean it differently? She knew that the worst thing that could happen now would be that he thought she fancied him, which of course she did, and if he acted on it because he felt he owed her something, or she expected it. That could ruin everything.

Feeling that she needed to test the situation and push things a little bit further to get some certainty, she got out of her office clothes and put on her dark grey jeans and the white linen shirt she never wore out of the house. The one where the top button was much lower than normal and left nothing to the imagination if she leaned even slightly forward, or as Mike had gleefully pointed out, if someone taller looked down at her.

In the kitchen the table was laid, wine glasses waited on the bench and the food cartons with their lids cut off sat in a row between their plates. 'I've got some better chopsticks than the ones they put in the bag,' she said and opened the drawer where she kept things that were rarely used. 'These lacquered, pointy ones that you can spear things with.'

She turned and held up the pointy chop sticks and the way Harry took in her shirt and quickly moved his eyes to meet hers told her everything. He did desire her, and he read the shirt message as if it was written on the front with black marker pen. For a long moment they just stared at each other, then she put the chop sticks on the table and sat down.

'Wow,' said Harry quietly, as if to himself, and sat down opposite. 'Well, let's celebrate, shall we?'

It made her laugh, that cool way he had of not saying the obvious, but making it clear he could read the situation. 'I bet you were good at dealing with the natives, so to speak, at those remote sites you mentioned.' She gave him a sly smile and he grinned but said nothing.

They talked about unimportant things over dinner, both reluctant to venture into anything remotely emotional, but throughout Abigail felt as if a slow fuse was invisibly and quietly smouldering. My God, she thought, and nearly made herself blush again, I haven't felt like this for a long, long time.

After tidying up they filled bowls with vanilla ice cream and went to the living room for more Baileys. They sat in the two armchairs where she and Mike had always sat, with the little glass table between them and their chairs half turned towards each other.

Suddenly a horrible thought struck Abigail, something she couldn't believe she hadn't thought about earlier. 'Oh no,' she exclaimed with her spoon halfway to her mouth. 'I never thought of this – what if you disappear to some other time and ...'

'Watch the spoon! It's just about to drip on that fabulous shirt and we don't want it ruined,' said Harry, his eyes once more focused on the top button. 'And me disappearing isn't likely, is it? It took being touched and burnt by ball lightning to get me here in the first place. I'll just stay inside during thunderstorms.'

'God, I hope so!' was all she said, and he gave her one of those looks, like when he first saw the shirt before dinner.

'I've been checking online for any mention of others who might have got flung out of the timestream when the ball of energy rolled through the terminal, but there's been nothing,' he said after a moment. 'I'm quite sure several other people were burnt by it, and a few people fell over at the far end of the terminal before the thing hit me. I thought maybe there would be a report of someone having turned up disorientated somewhere else in the country, but nothing so far.'

Abigail pointed her spoon at him again. 'But that's not surprising, is it? Think of it like this – you landed here in 2026, and we speculated that 2026 was kind of straight across a gap from 2029, as if the timestreams are parallel but out of sync timewise. Maybe that theory is wrong? Perhaps other people found themselves in other timestreams and in different years. Some might be in 2039 or something, and they might not all have appeared here, anyway, I mean in New Zealand. We'll never know.' She noticed his eyes on the spoon still suspended midair and laughed. 'Relax! This time I licked it first.'

Neither of them made any move of further

physical contact when they turned lights off and climbed the stairs, but Abigail felt their emotions mesh and tangle and knew that soon this connection would blossom, and it made her heart beat faster.

bigail smiled as she turned out of the driveway and heard the central locking automatically click into place. 'My old car didn't do that – Mike would have liked it. He always told me to engage the central locking as soon as I was in the car. He was obsessed with safety, sometimes tiresomely so. A side effect of his job, of course.'

They were driving down the curving road towards the business centre when Harry suddenly said, 'Could you stop here for a moment?'

They were right beside the pull-in parking area outside a primary school, and she stopped and waited for him to say something. After a long pause while he gazed at the school buildings he said, 'It's interesting that this school is so much bigger in this timestream – so many more classrooms and that big building that's a new hall or something. How many children attend this school, would you say?'

'Hang on a moment.' Abigail put the car in Park

mode and reached for her phone. 'Their website says 643. Why? How big is it in your time, do you think?'

'Probably no more than 250 or so. In my world there's only the main building and a smaller hall, probably only ten classrooms in total. What do you think caused the explosion of kids in this area?'

Abigail tried to think if anything much had changed, but as far as she knew this school had always looked more or less the same since she was a child. 'I don't think there's been any great increase. It's probably just the way some suburbs have a generation change and more young families move in. There are probably a couple of new classrooms but that's all. It might be because of the current trend for three or four children instead of just a couple the way it seemed to be for a couple of decades.'

'Three or four children?' said Harry disbelievingly. 'Well, here's another big difference - in my world you can only have two.'

'Really? How do they police that?' Abigail's thoughts went to China where for decades the leadership restricted family size. 'Do they penalise people who have more than two children through the tax system?'

'They do it in many ways,' said Harry and she could nearly feel him frowning even without looking at him. 'It's a hell of a system - if you have a third child your tax rate instantly goes up, that child doesn't get free healthcare, and of course everybody frowns at you in public. If you have a fourth kid you really hit the brick wall. Both of you end up with a court order for sterilisation and that poor fourth kid can't even go to school.'

Abigail sat in shocked silence for a long moment before she could think of anything to say. 'But what becomes of those number four kids? I mean, presumably their parents can teach them to read and write, but how far does that get them?'

'They become the labour force. The uneducated, hardworking people who have no privileges. There's another big group who become labourers and factory workers too, the least bright ones, who have to leave school at twelve. It's kept the population small for decades, so the need for new housing and bigger schools and hospitals is minimal, and now the only money spent on public facilities is for maintenance. Governments have been upfront about the reasons for decades now – they call it demographic stability, it's worldwide.'

Abigail pulled out into the traffic and negotiated two intersections without traffic lights in silence while she considered what Harry's world would be like to live in. For some reason she had never thought of the possibility that his world had developed so radically different from hers. It would be interesting to work out more exactly when things split apart, how long it had taken them in that timestream to develop such a divergence.

'But it won't work,' she said after a while. 'China tried it. You end up with a shrinking population if those who had kids only replace themselves. Lots can't or won't have children, so suddenly they're going to realise there aren't enough people to do the work and support the aging population.'

'I know – they just announced last year that so-called "elite" couples with high-performing kids would be paid to have one or two more. It was bound to happen.'

'Did you approve?' She asked finally and glanced sideways to see his expression. 'I mean, did you approve of the child restrictions?'

'No, not at all.' Harry's voice was hard and uncompromising. 'There were lots of things I didn't approve of, but I'd only ever risk talking about it with very close friends, who have the same opinions and know how to keep their mouths shut. It doesn't do you any good in my world to criticise the government. It affects your career and your employment prospects. And there's nothing you can do to change things, anyway.'

'Why can't people get together and try to change things?' Abigail though she knew what the reason was, she wanted to hear how he would explain it.

'I can't be done, it's impossible.' Harry sounded dejected. 'You can't form a protest group or organise demonstrations the way I'd read about people doing it here, but without social media and texting function on phones it's impossible. Word of mouth is too dangerous and doesn't have enough reach. And you can't start a new political party. The constitution says there can only be two parties –

and they're practically interchangeable, at least right now.'

After a few moments of silence while they approached the centre of the city he said, 'Could we drive around the business centre and out towards the hills? I would like to have a look at the high school I went to. I had to travel right across town to and from school every day. I was sent there by the authorities. If you were identified as so-called "academically gifted" you didn't have a choice of school – you had to go where you were sent.'

Hearing the tension in his voice, Abigail moved into the turning lane at the next intersection and set out for the suburb at the base of the high hills to the west of town. The hills had a light coating of snow and shone in the sun with the white-clad peaks of the Southern Alps as an impressive backdrop. She knew how to find the high school Harry had gone to; she had played in tennis tournaments there during her high school years. Harry sat for a long time looking at the brick buildings and the cricket field, immersed in thoughts he didn't share.

'Not very different,' he said finally. 'The main building looks more or less the same, but there are some new ones just behind it that I can't see properly - presumably new classrooms. But from here it's very recognisable. In my timestream I could go inside the main foyer and find myself in the photos of the top cricket team from my last two years of high school. I was their top bowler, and we won the regional championship both years I was in the First Eleven.'

On the way back through the suburbs, Abigail suddenly pulled into a vacant parking spot outside a shopping mall. 'Just wait here for a few minutes, please. I just thought of something.'

She ran across the road to the menswear store she had noticed and returned with a paper carrier bag, which she handed to Harry before she pulled out into the traffic again. 'A present for you.'

'Underpants!' he exclaimed. 'My God, you think of everything. I've been wearing Mike's lightweight swim shorts under my jeans.'

'I just remembered this morning that I threw all Mike's out. I only bought four pairs in case you don't like that style.'

'They're perfect – thank you!'

Very early on Saturday morning Abigail woke up when Harry bounded up the stairs, taking two or three steps at a time as he always did. She looked blurrily at the alarm clock on her bedside table. 'Half past *four*!' she exclaimed. 'What *is* he doing up at this hour?'

Harry heard her and came to stand in the door to her bedroom, and though her light wasn't on she could see he was dressed. 'Sorry! I didn't mean to wake you, but I've had a great idea for earning money, which is important because I don't have any.'

Abigail sat up and turned the bedside light on. Too late she noticed Harry's eyes taking in her strappy satin nightdress - soft and slippery and probably showing more than she realised. *Don't look down to check what he can see!* she told herself. *Just act cool, pretend you don't care.* 'Are you going to tell me what this idea is?'

He dragged his eyes away from her breasts and looked a bit embarrassed, but all he said was, 'Titanium!'

'Oh, for God's sake, please don't be mysterious at this time of the morning, or the night, or whatever half past four is. Come in and tell me properly.'

'Are you sure?' She could tell he felt embarrassed at having stared. 'Maybe we should talk later?'

She had to laugh and for once she wasn't blushing. Who did he think he was he kidding? 'It's too late - you've seen it now, so let's forget about that. Come and sit down on the bed and let me have the full story. Something to do with titanium – like what you went to explore in Brazil. This sounds interesting.'

He sat half sideways at the foot end of the bed on Mike's side, so he could look at her, but also so he wasn't close, and she knew why. This was exactly the kind of situation that might get out of hand and turn into rampant sex, and she didn't know if either of them was ready for that yet. In an instant she recalled the way his hands felt on her back the night he woke her from the nightmare, the knuckle kiss and the day he ran his finger down her cheek when she blushed, and she shivered as a hot line of desire ran down her body. If he did that now, she would probably grab him and drag him down beside her.

'I went downstairs to check online if that site in Brazil is being mined in this timestream. I just came up to get a sweater, the thermostat is still on the night setting. The site I located is going to be one of the biggest finds ever, provided what we discovered in 2029 is right which I'm sure it is, and if it hasn't been mined yet, I might be able to sell the information to some big mining company that specialises in titanium. I could tell them I've done some private work out there, and I can give them a rough estimate of the potential yield, and I'd only tell them where it is if they pay me. I'd have to set up a waterproof contract.'

'If you say it's in Brazil, won't they guess where it might be?'

'God no, Brazil is huge, and that site is nowhere near where anyone in my timestream had ever thought of looking before – quite a weird location.'

'Did you try Google Earth? Remember the icon on my desktop I showed you with the blue and white globe – we opened it, and I showed you how to search for a location. That might show you something useful.' She thought for a moment. Was there anything else that might be useful? 'Oh, and on the Google Earth images there's usually a date at the bottom of the screen that tells you when the satellite image was taken, and you can zoom in for a closer look.'

'Right! I'd forgotten that Earth thing – I'll check it out straight away.'

She knew he was dying to go downstairs again and continue his search, but this was intriguing. 'How come you went looking just there? Had the company you worked for identified the site?'

'No, I did that. I'd discovered a while back that

the really big titanium finds were in areas that has certain geological features in common. Not major things, nothing obvious, just little trace elements in certain combinations, so I started analysing these and came up with a kind of formula or a template, I suppose you could call it. And in this case that template led to a major find.' He gave her a wry smile. 'That doesn't mean it hasn't already been discovered in this timestream, of course, but it's worth checking.'

She stared at him while a whirl of thoughts and ideas turned over in her mind, then she said mock-seriously, 'And then you'll be wealthy, and you'll be able to take me out for dinner at that fabulous luxury lodge high up in the western hills, that Mountain View place – I've never been there. Or better still, we could spend a whole weekend there in a luxury suite and have delicious food three times a day and be waited on hand and foot.'

She was joking, but she heard the underlying seriousness in his voice when he replied in an off-hand way, as if he was joking too. 'Anything you desire – your wish is my command. If I get some money and you want roast hummingbird, I'll get it for you.'

'Perfect!' She yawned, slid down in the bed and reached out to turn the bedside light off. 'I'll see you later - I refuse start my day this early.'

He came around the bed in the half dark with only the vague light from the hallway coming in the open door, bent down and kissed her forehead, and left.

She lay there, half drowsing and thought of the last few days, the little signposts along the way that all pointed in the same direction. She had never known anyone like Harry before, she hadn't even realised a man could be like that. To be able to wait and just leave those little touch messages without taking the next step. It's delicious, she thought and smiled in the dark, it's like every touch is a little promise of more deliciousness to come, very laid-back and moving slowly forward. And the way she could read those looks of his, when his eyes fastened on hers or on some part of her body, the way he quietly said "wow" when she came down in the shirt that buttoned too low.

When Abigail came downstairs at a more normal time, the washing machine was on, and Harry was sitting at the end of the kitchen table with both laptops in front of him. He had a sheet of paper ripped from her notebook in his hand, a pen clamped between his teeth and a sheaf of notes beside him.

She stood for a moment watching him, fascinated by this new insight into his personality. The intense focus on what he was doing was like a forcefield around him, so instead of talking she made coffee and toast as quietly as possible. When she put a plate beside his mug of coffee with two slices of toast with peanut butter he didn't even notice.

Abigail smiled and headed for the living room with her own breakfast and sat down to read. Two hours later Harry appeared in the doorway and said triumphantly, 'Right! It's good news so far. Do you want to hear?'

'Are you crazy? Of course I do! Sit down and tell me what you've found.'

'No, you come with me. Come along! Let's have some more coffee and some of those almond biscuits – this is exciting, we need to celebrate.'

'OK,' said Harry ten minutes later. 'This is what I've been able to dig up - pun intended - and it looks promising. I can find no evidence that any prospecting or excavating has taken place at that site. The Google Earth image was taken in November 2025 and there's no sign that any prospecting's been done. I know exactly where to look, of course, and there's no sign of a temporary camp, no ground cleared, no track bulldozed in - nothing! As far as I can find out the Brazilian authorities haven't granted any prospecting rights, but that doesn't mean much. Who knows what goes on behind the scenes? And there are no articles about that region in geological journals, and it would have been written about, I'm sure. Even a rumour would have been reported on, such an unlikely part of Bazil to even look at. How about that?!'

Abigail pulled the packet towards her, took an

almond biscuits and bit into it while she processed this and tried to imagine what the next step would be. And more importantly, how this must be taken into account when Jasper came.

'There are several things we must do,' she said finally. 'We must ask Jasper if he can establish you as a geologist, so you have credibility, or else you'll have to come up with a good story to explain how you were able to discover this. I mean to someone you're trying to sell the idea to. And we'll have to find some specialist kind of lawyer, who knows about the sort of contract you'll need to safeguard your interests. What have I left out?'

Harry chuckled. 'Within one minute you've grasped all the key elements – not that I expected anything less. What I must do right away is write it up like a report with facts and figures. I think all the data is still in my head – thank God that ball lightning didn't wipe my memory!'

Abigail took another bite of her biscuit and chewed thoughtfully while she tried to picture how this process of many steps would play out. 'And you obviously won't tell them which region of Brazil it is, will you? Even if it's huge and they don't know the exact spot. But will you reveal your template thing in the report? They might just hijack it and use it for themselves.'

'No, but I can say that I've worked out a kind of key to where to find titanium and that it's proved its value in the past, and that's how I've identified the site. I can give them enough hints in technical language, so they understand the basics behind it, but I won't reveal what those little geological puzzle pieces are.'

Suddenly Abigail thought of something neither of them had mentioned so far. 'A patent! Apply for a patent for your template! Then people have to pay to use it and you'll be famous.'

He got up and stretched. 'No patents, I don't think. Getting famous is the last thing I want. However clever Jasper is, I think I'd prefer to stay under the radar. I'm going to have a shower now.'

Abigail took the washing out of the machine and put it in the dryer before she called Astrid. Mentioning Jasper had made her realise that if Harry was going to tell Astrid more about his dystopian 2029, then she and Jasper might as well hear it at the same time.

'Dinner here on Wednesday night,' she said when Astrid picked up the call. 'Jasper will be here by mid-afternoon, and you can have the pleasure of watching him watch that video clip, which is how we'll convince him to believe Harry's story. And then Harry can tell both of you about life in his timestream, so he doesn't have to repeat it more than once.'

'Great! I'll bring dessert,' said Astrid, who never cooked anything that resembled a real meal and seemed to live on soup and eggs, but who was very good at making lovely desserts.

By mid-morning on Wednesday the kitchen had already been busy for a couple of hours. A lamb casserole with button mushrooms and root ginger was simmering on low heat in a cast iron pot on the stove, soon be turned off and left to cool. Potatoes a la Hasselback, sliced thinly nearly right through, sat in a bowl of water, ready to be roasted and liberally basted with melted butter, and Abigail was tidying up the mess she before heading upstairs to change.

'There!' she said and went to throw two towels in the bin in the laundry room. 'I'll go and have a shower now.'

Harry looked up from his laptop. 'Anything I can help you with?' and Abigail said coolly, 'No thanks, I think I can wash and dress myself.'

She heard his chuckle as she left the kitchen and switched her thoughts from the nearly irresistible idea of having a shower with Harry to the coming afternoon and evening. Astrid had texted and said she had asked if she could leave work a couple of hours early, so she could be there when Jasper arrived, to be there, as she put it, when the fun started.

Unbeknownst to Harry, Abigail had compiled a list of things they must remember to tell or ask Jasper, and also things Harry had told her about his timestream, background which might get left out when he told his story. So much detail now, she thought when she stripped her clothes off in the bathroom, so many aspects that need to be covered. Even things that might seem unimportant could turn out to be important later, so they must tell Jasper absolutely everything.

When she came down dressed in one of her favourite pale blue shirts and jeans, Harry had tidied up his papers and moved both laptops to the far end of the table. 'Isn't it lucky the kitchen is big enough for a large table? You look very pretty! There's no rush - don't you want to dry your hair before we have coffee?'

'I usually just leave it.' She ran her fingers through her mass of loose blond curls. 'It's hopeless hair. I could use the straightener, but it takes forever, so I hardly ever bother.'

'Shit, no - please don't straighten it! Not ever,' said Harry. 'I love your hair just as it is. It felt so nice when I ...' He stopped and she knew why. He was thinking of the sushi incident when he held her tight and ran his hand up through her hair and clasped the back of her head to hold her against him.

They looked at each other for a long moment, then Abigail smiled. 'It was nice for me too,' she said lightly and went to the fridge to get the milk,

'Does Harry want to read The Time Traveller's Wife? I could bring a copy.' texted Astrid.

Without consulting him Abigail replied, *'Great idea! I won't even ask him. Can you take it on extended loan please, don't know when he'll get to it, flat out working on geology stuff.'*

The day seemed to move slowly. With Harry busy re-constructing his report about the findings in Brazil and dinner prepared far too early there was nothing for Abigail to do and she felt restless.

Her week off had been booked a couple of months ago, and she had planned to visit friends in Wellington and Napier, but Harry's arrival had changed all that. Her phone call to Rosemary, to tell her she wouldn't come after all, had presented her with a problem. She didn't want to tell Rosemary about Harry living in the house yet, and certainly not how he had arrived, so she didn't mention him. Would Rosemary get upset, she wondered, if Abigail did what people called *moved on* from her grief over Mike's death? Would she feel it was too soon? Mike had always said Rosemary was the only member of his family he was close to, but it had sometimes seemed to Abigail that Rosemary didn't share that feeling, that she had actually become closer to herself than to Mike. She made an excuse about postponing her week off due to sickness at work and left the issue of telling Rosemary about Harry to be tackled later.

After lunch Abigail studied the now tidy kitchen and shook her head at her own behaviour. 'I always do this, I don't know why, it's ridiculous - I do things far too early, like a compulsive urge to never get caught with something left too late. And then it's all done, and I can't think what to do with myself until later.'

'Maybe we could use the time to organise that wine cupboard in the garage,' said Harry sounding slightly cautious. 'You've asked me to get something a couple of times, and there's no system – the different types of wine are mixed up, so you end up pulling out a dozen bottles to find what you're after.' He looked carefully at her. 'It's not a criticism of Mike, just a thought I had.'

'Great idea – let's do that. It's very irritating. I like things to be very tidy, as you know. Mike and I had very different versions of the tidiness gene. He used to say I've got a double copy of it, but that was just a way of excusing that he was untidy by nature, very untidy.'

Harry's hesitation, his reluctance to imply any criticism of Mike was a nice trait, she thought, but there was no need for it. They had some characteristics in common, but in the main they were radically different. Harry's slow-burn approach to their mutual attraction was the absolute opposite of Mike's way of conducting their initial romance, which had been more like a crusader storming a citadel. It made her smile to imagine them side by side in her mind; Mike slightly stocky, grizzled, always direct and prone to being over-protective, and Harry, leaner, handsome and with an unusual way of dealing with women, or at least with her.

Sorting out the wine cupboard took longer than either of them had anticipated. They took the several dozen bottles from the racks in the cupboard and sat them on the floor in groups according to type of wine, and as Abigail said, that was the easy part. Deciding how to put them back and where to leave empty slots proved harder. After a rather frustrating discussion, Harry said patiently, 'Let's have a row of empty slots between each type and then we can add new ones after or before when we buy them, according to what's been used and ...' Then he stopped abruptly and added in completely different tone of voice, 'I mean you could do that, not "we" – I'm sorry! I'm not taking anything for granted, Abigail.'

The way he looked at her nearly made her smile, but she kept a straight face. Talk about getting caught with your hand in the cookie jar, she thought, but all she said was, 'Saying "we" works for me – and your idea is good. Let's do it that way.'

. . .

'Look at you, you pretty thing!' said Jasper half an hour later and dropped his bag on the floor. He enveloped her in one of his usual bear hugs, which due to his height squashed her face flat against his chest. 'I was offered a seat on an earlier flight, but I forgot to text and say I was coming an hour early, so I killed some time in the airport cafe.'

He handed her a bag, noticed Harry standing in the door to the kitchen and reached out to shake hands. 'This is Harry, Jasper,' said Abigail. 'He's the other half of the "we" I mentioned when I called.' She looked in the bag and laughed. 'Great choice! A bag full of almond croissants, my favourite pastry. Let's make coffee – no wait, you don't drink coffee. Tea?'

'Yes please, and strong, I hope you still remember how to make Yorkshire tea.'

She could see he was sizing Harry up and thought how much she looked forward to showing him the video, but she had promised Astrid to let her watch Jasper's reaction, so she said quite casually that they would have a drink and a pastry first, before they got down to business.

But Astrid arrived earlier than expected, rosy cheeked and rushed, took one look at Jasper and exclaimed, 'Oh no! He didn't watch it already, did he?'

Jasper stared, Harry laughed, and Abigail said, 'Darling, calm down! Jasper, this is my sister Astrid who is often unable to control her impulses. She meant to say hi first, but some urgent thought interrupted. She is very excited to meet you, but not for any reason you know yet. Let's do it, shall we?'

Harry quietly and without fuss set Abigail's laptop in front of Jasper, directed Astrid with just a look and a nod to sit opposite and turned to help Abigail put mugs on the table. She put the plate of almond croissants in the middle of the table and bending down beside Jasper she pulled the laptop slightly towards her.

'There's something we want you to watch before we tell you about our problem. I know you're wondering about this setup, but you'll understand in a minute.' She pointed at the file. 'This is a clip from my security camera. Play it and tell us what you think.'

Probably nobody's ever been so closely watched by three people while watching a three minute video clip, she thought, amused and expectant. By now she knew without looking how long it took until Harry materialised on the front lawn, and a second after that point Jasper jerked and sat up straight. 'What the fuck!'

Astrid burst out laughing. 'Exactly! Isn't it incredible?'

'How the hell did you do that?' Jasper looked suspiciously at Harry. 'Is it some kind of new parkour stunt? But naked, and in snow?'

Abigail could see how taken aback Harry was by the question and intervened. 'No, it's not a stunt! Would you please start the recording again and continue right through? And pay particular attention to both the time stamp and to the lack of footprints in the snow. And *then* we'll talk about it.'

'OK,' said Jasper meekly. 'Sorry! I was just so startled. Make me another cup of tea or something stronger, please. I think I'm going to need it.'

With Astrid watching him closely, Jasper spent quarter of an hour going back and forth in the video, and the more he watched it the deeper the creases between his eyebrows became. Finally, he emptied the second cup of tea Abigail had set beside him in one gulp and shook his head, his gaze moving from Abigail to Harry and back again.

'Right! This is incredible – I haven't got a clue what this is about, but I think we need to break out the beer right now! Before you even start explaining.' He pointed at Astrid. 'I can see what *you* were so excited about. Did they show you this without any lead-in, too? Did they sit there and watch you watching it, just loving your reactions?'

'And I did exactly the same thing you did. I went through it about three times and kept stopping it to check details. The most incredible thing ever!'

Abigail got up and Harry joined her while Astrid and Jasper continued talking about the video. 'Please see if you can stop her telling him where you're from, she's so excited now,' whispered Abigail to Harry with her back to the table, standing on tiptoes and leaning close so Jasper wouldn't hear.

Harry moved closer still and rested his forehead against hers for a moment and she had to stop herself from reaching up to touch him. 'OK – I'll divert her for a moment.' He turned and said, 'Hey, Astrid, could you help me choose a couple of wines for dinner while Abigail gets glasses and some snacks out?'

'Snacks? We've just had pastries,' said Abigail to their retreating backs as they disappeared through the door to the garage. 'But why not? I hope I bought the right beer, Jasper – I think I recognised the cans in the supermarket.'

She put a beer can in front of Jasper and went to

put chips and nuts in bowls. When she turned he was quietly watching the video again with a look of intense concentration and she laughed. 'Checking the time stamps again? We all have – well, Harry and I don't need to. We know it's real, but we did it anyway to make sure nobody could say it's been edited. Not that we're planning to show anyone else, it's just for us four.'

'OK,' said Abigail and looked seriously at Jasper. 'It's going to take a bit of time to tell you about his, because a story of many parts, and I know you'll have lots of questions, just like Astrid did. We asked her to come back, so she could hear more detail than what we told her the other night. But I think we must try to tell you the whole thing before you start asking for details or we'll get sidetracked and nothing will make sense. And let's face it, some parts might never make sense however hard we try.'

She paused and looked at Harry and thought that perhaps she should have mentioned this to him earlier. 'I had an idea while you were working on your report this morning and then I forgot. Would you mind if we tell it chronologically? So, I start with it from my point of view that night and we kind of take turns from there?'

'OK, much better than going around in circles. And then at the end I can explain more of … where I came from.'

Jasper's attention on them was now so intense it felt like an interrogation, thought Abigail, and smiled at him. She picked up her phone, put it in the middle of the table and set it to record.

'So, here's how it started. I was sitting up late watching TV, not last Friday night, the one before, and just before midnight I heard someone turn the front door handle. I checked through the peephole and outside stood a naked man, shivering with cold and looking totally exhausted. When I opened the door he collapsed half inside and then he passed out. The only thing he had time to say was, "what are you doing in my house?" And then ...'

She continued with how she wrapped Harry in a warm rug and checked his pulse and then sat in the chair watching him until he finally woke up at five in the morning.

She nodded at Harry, who continued from there with how he dressed in Mike's clothes, which she had got out for him while he slept, and the strange and disjointed conversation they had over hot chocolate at the kitchen table as they tried to get their bearings.

'The strangest thing, though, and it struck me even at that early stage, was how calm she was.' He moved his head slowly from side to side. 'Unbelievable! No hysterics, no disbelief when I explained I came from 2029 – which we got to when I noticed her phone had 2026 on the lock screen.'

There was a gasp of surprise from Jasper, but Harry continued without stopping. 'So, we had a bit of a discussion about that, and about how I could prove a knew every inch of this house and that I'd lived in it for several years in another ... era. Some of those years concurrent with her and Mike's years in this same house in this era. And then she got her laptop, and we checked the video from the security camera, which you've just watched, and then she started asking questions.'

He smiled at the expression on Jasper's face. 'It took a little while to work out that I wasn't from her future, that I was from a separate timestream, so things got quite intense, very complicated.' He pulled his sweatshirt sleeve up and showed them the long, shiny burn scar that went from his elbow to his wrist

'This is part of what I think caused this strange thing, the way I got shifted to this timestream – and yes, I can see your questions lining up, Jasper, but just hang on. I'd just come back from Brazil where I'd been on a job for a couple of weeks. I was at the airport in Auckland waiting for my connecting flight down here when all hell broke loose.'

The story of the ball lightning had his audience mesmerised. Abigail couldn't tell whose eyes were open widest, Jasper's or Astrid's. Ah, we never told her this bit, she thought and listened to the exclamations and questions about the scene in the airport terminal. There are going to be a lot of surprises in the next hour or two.

After initially responding to the barrage of questions, Harry pulled them back to the story. 'Listen, we can go into details about the physics of ball lightning later, let's just continue on the timeline for now, so we can get it into a sequence that makes sense.'

He sent a sideways look at Astrid, who was just about to ask yet another question, and she closed her mouth and said nothing. 'So, between Abigail and myself, we've decided to call our separate existences timestreams for lack of a better word. We think of them as parallel but out of sync timewise and possibly having branched off more than once. We'll never know for certain, but we assume I was somehow flicked me into this timestream when the ball lightning zapped me - not physically, but a cloned version.'

He included the details of how they found that he didn't exist in the here and now, that he had never been born and consequently had no background. 'In this world, my father didn't marry my mother or even have the same job,' he said with a wry smile. 'He married a woman I've never heard about, but his birth date was the same. We found their wedding photo online – definitely him. There are so many things that are impossible to get a handle on. Like if the man, who isn't my father here, has children – are they still my half siblings?' He shook his head. 'But exactly when things split apart and how many versions there are, we have no idea, of course.'

At the end of an hour, they had heard the entire story and debated some of the conclusions Abigail and Harry had reached. Abigail had detailed the research they had done and what they had speculated about, like whether Harry now existed in two separate timestreams. Or had he been deposited in their timestream and simply vanished from the one he'd been in? Harry briefly described what the report was about, the one he was writing from memory, and why, which made Jasper's eyes open wide with surprise.

'Jesus!' he said and got up to get a third can of beer out of the fridge. 'I'm glad you thought of recording this – so much info. It's the most amazing thing I've ever heard! If anyone else had told me this I would have brushed it off as a joke. And this opportunity with the titanium find - incredible! It will be very interesting to see how that works out, but it will have to be managed very carefully, of course. I'm not sure if I can be of any help there but just ask if you think of something I can do.'

When a new discussion started about how to safeguard Harry's knowledge about the site in Brazil, Abigail got up and turned the casserole on to reheat, spooned melted butter over the potatoes she had put in the oven earlier and retreated to the hall to quietly do a mental recap of her list. Only two things from Harry's background had not been covered: his marriage, which he might prefer not to mention, and the restrictions on how many children a couple was allowed in his timestream.

She returned to the kitchen just in time to hear Astrid reverting to what he had told them about the changes in world government and the restrictive world he had lived in. 'Unbelievable!' she said. 'Like some horrible dystopian film, so depressing!'

'And I don't think you've even heard about the child restrictions yet, that's truly scary,' said Abigail and started getting plates and cutlery out while she listened to Harry telling them how it worked in his world.

'Some of it's a bit like that book, *1984*,' said Jasper, 'and some is even worse. My God! I know you've lost your family and all that, but I hope the differences here make up for some of it.'

Harry nodded. 'Precisely! And now I think I'll go upstairs and put on a short sleeved t-shirt – this kitchen's getting hot.'

Abigail could feel his need to escape for a few minutes, to get away from intense questions and endless explanations. She slipped out behind him, leaving Jasper and Astrid to an animated discussion about Harry's timestream, and caught up with Harry in the upstairs hall where he was standing motionless, as if lost, just beside his bedroom door. She put her arms around him from behind and leaned her forehead against his back.

'Too much pressure down there?'

He turned in her arms and pulled her close. 'Just a bit overwhelming to go through it all in one go like that, yes. But I'm OK – I just needed to step away from all the questions for a few minutes.' He ran one hand up through her hair and smiled down at her upturned face. 'You read me like a book, every time!'

She kissed his chin, gently freed herself and took a step back saying, 'Don't forget the short sleeved t-shirt!' over her shoulder before she ran down the stairs again. I can play this slow-burn game too, she thought. Let's see who makes that crucial last move and ignites the explosive charge. This is such fun, I've never done it before.

Over dinner the initial excitement died down and as they ate the conversation gradually became calmer. Jasper clearly found Astrid both funny and clever and kept her questions about his job at bay by teasing her. 'I saw you blush a minute ago, so don't you try to put me off,' he said when she once again protested she didn't have a boyfriend. 'You can't trick me - you've fallen in love, haven't you? I know the signs, I have heaps more experience than you do. Come on, tell us who he is – or is it a girl?'

'Don't be silly! I'm not in love - I'm over all that stuff. It takes up too much time and energy. You're only trying to distract me, aren't you?'

It made Abigail laugh to hear them bickering, Jasper teasing and Astrid being evasive. She thought of Astrid's close relationship with Mike and once again realised what a gap his death had left in her sister's life. The loss of that steadying influence and the voice of reason, and not least the affection and support of a grown man. For a girl whose early life had had lacked any father type relationship, her close bond with Mike had been invaluable.

Now she watched Astrid interact with Jasper and then in response to Harry's slight nod, get up and help him dish out ice cream into bowls and after a whispered conversation go and fetch the bottle of Bayley's from the living room cabinet. They've formed a little relationship already, she thought and put the last dinner plates in the dishwasher. She trusts him or she wouldn't be so responsive to directions. He's much quieter and calmer than Mike's more robust approach. Maybe her relationship with Harry will be more one of equals, two adults, rather than one between Mike and Astrid that started out as a hesitant friendship between a child and a grown man.

It was late when Jasper hugged Abigail and left in a taxi to go to his hotel, but Astrid stayed half an hour longer in the hope of discovering from Abigail what Jasper's job was. She left disappointed after assuring them that she had truly only had one glass of wine, and she was fine to drive. Abigail closed the door behind her and checked the lock, feeling suddenly exhausted.

'That went quite well, I think. And if you wondered about that whispered conversation with Astrid, it was just her telling me she forgot to bring the dessert she made – too excited and in a hurry to get here.' Harry yawned. 'Is it bedtime yet? I'm tired.'

At quarter to six in the morning, a phone call from Jasper woke Abigail. 'Sorry about this! I've had an urgent request from work to come back asap, so I must cut this visit short. Would it be OK if I come over in forty-five minutes?'

'Of course – we'll have breakfast ready when you get here. What time is your flight?'

'The earliest one I could get leaves at quarter to two, so if I leave your place an hour before that I should make it, no problems – I only have hand luggage.'

An hour later he dropped his bag on the hall floor and shrugged out of his jacket. 'My God – I'm sure that wind comes straight off the Antarctic ice cap. The snow's blowing sideways, and the taxi was slipping and sliding. The driver said yesterday's damp roads have turned to black ice all over town.'

'Just a normal winter,' said Abigail, after hanging up his jacket and giving him a hug. As she walked ahead of him to the kitchen where the breakfast things were ready and waiting, she added, 'Harry's just getting dressed, I think. He was having a shower when I came down. Sit down and have a cup of tea while I get some toast going.'

And just saying that, such an ordinary thing to say, suddenly made her feelings for Harry real in a nearly tangible way and gave her a sense of belonging. To say she knew exactly what he was doing, not to mention that she could, of course, picture him in the shower having seen him naked - it felt real. She wasn't just falling into love or lust; this was more endurable than that. Is there such a thing as forever-after love? she wondered.

'Morning!' Harry appeared in the doorway in a short sleeved t-shirt and saw Jasper's look. 'Isn't it lucky this house has such great central heating?'

Abigail, who had her back turned, jumped at the sound of his voice, and said accusingly, 'Are you sneaking up on me now? I didn't hear you come bouncing down the stairs.'

'Socks!' He pointed at his feet. 'And how come you're here so early, Jasper?'

'They want me back urgently - there's some kind of emergency, could be anything. There was nothing special going on when I left.' Jasper yawned and took the piece of toast Abigail handed him. 'But the kind of trouble I deal with is often invisible in media — backroom threats that often happen lightning fast.' He yawned again. 'Sorry – but it's time to get serious, guys. What I want us to do first up is compile a list of priorities. I was thinking about this situation last night, and we've got to do this in the right order. So let's start with the name – what's your surname, Harry?'

'Hipkins – Harold Hipkins, no middle name.'

'OK, let's keep the Harold/Harry bit, but we need something less memorable for a last name, some common surname.'

'Williams is the most common, after Singh, Smith and Patel.' Abigail tried not to smile at the surprised faces turned her way.

'Singh and Patel! Really?' Jasper laughed. 'I would never have guessed – how do you know?'

'You know what a ragbag of random information my brain is,' said Abigail lightly. 'Full of scraps of facts nobody needs. But seriously, I looked it up the other day when I was thinking about what we might need to do.'

'Ha! Ragbag! More like a depository of vital data.' Harry turned to Jasper and said seriously, 'I've never met anyone so deceptive in my life. When I woke up on the hall floor that morning wrapped up like a mummy, this harmless-looking, pretty woman calmly took charge, untangled me and got me on my feet, told me to get dressed and went to make hot chocolate and breakfast. No indication of fear or embarrassment, and she never lost her cool for one second from then on. Well, just once or twice, I think, but nothing major.'

He slanted a glance Abigail's way, and she knew he was teasing, referring to her occasional blushes.

'You're not telling me anything I didn't already know. She's always been like that and if it wasn't for what she calls *the curse of the true blond* we'd never know.' Jasper grinned. 'Like right now – just look at that blush!'

'Stop it, you two! I refuse to be teased at this time of the morning. I think Harry Williams is a good name – or we could pick one that begins like Hipkins in case he starts saying the wrong name. Maybe Hislop or something.'

'No, I like Williams,' said Harry and watched Jasper write it on the note pad he had left on the table last night. 'And let's forget Harold – horrible name. We'll just stick with Harry.'

And hour later the list had grown and was being re-prioritised. 'Some things are kind of given,' said Jasper. 'Like name and date of birth, that's the first building block, and is a good one too, but let's not forget place of birth. It would be ideal to make it New Zealand, if I can tweak the data, but I don't think even I can do it. And then we'll have to decide on a university, but not one in this country. It would be too hard to filter in an extra graduate without anyone noticing. I mean, nobody would have any recollection of you, and it's not a subject that has thousands of students, is it? Let's have you go to one overseas, a big one, but not ivy league. You can decide which one, Harry.'

They continued discussing and occasionally debating until Jasper put his pen down an hour later and held up the pad. 'This mess of arrows and numbers and crossed out stuff, is now the master plan I'll be working on. I'll do it from my computer at home – I've got a DMZ, a demilitarized zone, around my gear, so it's pretty untraceable. This messy flowchart seems pretty good as a starting point. How do you feel about being listed with "father unknown" in the records so it doesn't involve someone who's alive and kicking in this timestream?'

Harry drank the last of his now cold coffee and got up with the mug in his hand. 'Does anyone want another cup? I'll make it.'

'Mine's tea and leave the teabag in my mug, please, and the spoon,' said Jasper and made another note on his pad. 'I'm really pleased you recorded everything last night, Abby. Give me the recording on a USB stick – I'll keep it safe.'

'I have nothing against not knowing who my father was,' said Harry, 'and if we pick a common woman's name for my fictitious mother, call her something like Anne Williams or whatever fits the era when I was born, then it's all innocuous. And I must start working on a personal background in case I get asked where I went to school or which street I lived in, but I'll wait until you tell me where you decide I was born. But let's forget about the degree, much better that I'm a university drop-out.'

He put the mugs of coffee and tea on the table, one after the other, and smiled at their surprised faces, but they soon understood the advantage of him being a drop-out.

'Of course!' Abigail nodded. 'That way there's no problem if someone tries to check your degree – much safer. And it gives you the background knowledge about why and where to do the prospecting and how to write the report.'

'Precisely!' Harry smiled at Jasper, who was looking absently into the middle distance and seemed to not be listening. 'What's up Jasper? Something worrying you?'

'Passport,' he said briefly. 'Driver's licence is easy, you just go into the nearest AA office, and they'll take a photo. I'll give you what you need to prove you are who you say you are, but the passport issue is tricky. They've put some safeguards in place – well, we did it, actually – and I don't think I dare try to get around them. We set up high density firewalls that react instantly to breach attempts, so it's probably doomed. Hackers had been selling fake licences to people who used them for ID – even got them into the system so they worked if the cops checked them. But no more, impossible now.'

They looked at each other for a long moment, then Harry said casually, 'Forget the passport, then, let's just leave it out. I don't need to go anywhere. To tell you the truth, I'd rather not set foot in an airport terminal again in my life. Don't forget what happened last time.'

Jasper lifted and dipped the teabag several times, still with a frown-creases between his eyebrows and they all watched as the tea in hug mug got darker and darker. 'You could tan leather with it now,' said

Abigail quietly to Harry. 'God knows what his insides look like, probably pitch black.'

'What if you find a taker for that info about the titanium site and they want you to fly to the US or Russia or something to discuss it, or they might want you at the actual site in Brazil? Without a passport you're locked in place here.'

But Harry just shrugged. 'Medical,' he said briefly. 'Some waterproof reason why I can't fly. I'll just say I might never be able to fly again. When they realise the size of the find and how unlikely it is that they'll discover where it is, they'll just send a team here if they want to discuss it face-to-face.'

He saw their expressions of slight disbelief and said decisively, 'You two just don't understand the magnitude of this find – I can see it from the look on your faces right now. But believe me, the impact of this will be immense, and it will make headlines on the financial pages around the globe. Some company will be able to assume world domination and control the market for titanium anode batteries. Don't forget I come from a place where *everything*, literally everything, runs on batteries. Trucks, trains, heavy machinery, ships, and planes.'

Jasper sat up straighter and stared at him. 'Christ! Everything? I didn't realise when you told us what your world was like – I only thought of cars and maybe trucks.'

'We'll just have to find a perfect health problem for you. I'll do some research,' said Abigail. 'Now I've got to call Astrid and tell her tonight's dinner won't be including you, Jasper. She texted this morning and said she was looking forward to bringing the dessert she made for last night and forgot to bring.'

Abigail left the men in the kitchen and went to sit in the living room. Right now was probably the right time for Astrid to have time to chat after the early morning chores in the library. But before she had even unlocked her phone, Astrid called her.

'Listen!' she said urgently, talking very fast. 'It's just possible that Aaron might be on his way to your place. He was in here not two minutes ago, just after we opened, and he made a point of finding me. I'm working in the children's department today, so he couldn't pretend it was just chance he saw me, but he was asking about Harry!'

'Oh shit!' said Abigail without thinking and heard Astrid giggle. 'What did he ask?'

'He asked if I knew Harry, so I said "of course I know Harry! He's a family friend. Why are you asking about him?" and then he said he was just interested, and he'd never heard Mike mention him and what was his surname.'

'And?'

'Well, first I said, I've no idea what his surname is, I've just always called him Harry. And I used that story you and Harry made up when he came the day you cut your finger that you told me about, and thank goodness you did, so I said you and Mike used to have skiing holidays with him. And then I got angry, so I said "and *precisely why* are you coming in here all the time asking about Abigial? It's creepy! And it's not as if you know any of our family friends, is it? You were never part of the family. Are you stalking Abigail?'

'God, you're a star! I can't thank you enough – I must go back to the kitchen and warn the guys. And Jasper's flying back to Wellington later today, he's got to get back for some urgent issue that just cropped up at his work. But come for dinner – and don't forget that dessert!'

'Hey, guys,' said Abigail and they stopped talking at the tone of her voice. 'This little problem needs thinking about right now. I don't know if I'm panicking or … Listen to what Astrid just told me.'

She related the whole story including Astrid's replies to Aaron and relaxed a bit when both men laughed. 'That girl!' said Jasper. 'What a treasure she is! But don't worry, I'll deal with this.'

'How?' Harry frowned. 'I thought I would open the door if he comes and give him a strong message to stay away.'

'Yeah, but think how baffled he'll be, if yet another male is in the house now. He won't know what to think, will he? If Astrid didn't mention me, I can first give him a surprise and then send him on his way. You can listen from here, but don't let him see you, if he does come, because my brain just spawned a great idea.'

27

They had just started clearing up the mess on the table for an early lunch when there was a knock on the door and Abigail jumped. 'That's him!'

Jasper went into the front hall leaving the kitchen door half open, and they heard him open the front door. 'Yes?' he said politely, the way anyone might when a presumably innocent stranger knocks on the door. 'Can I help you?'

There was a moment of silence before Aaron got his thoughts together. Abigail imagined the cogs moving in his head: another strange man in her house, another potential competitor? 'Hi, is Abigail here?'

'Well, kind of. No, I mean she's here, but she's not available right now.'

Abigail's eyes met Harry's and moved her head slowly from side to side and mouthed "what?!" Harry grinned.

Aaron's voice took on the kind of tone Abigail imagined he used when interviewing suspects, harder, as if he demanded an answer. 'And what does that mean? Is she all right? And who are you?'

'I'm James, a long-time friend of Abigail's and a guest in this house! And who the hell are you, yourself? Show some manners and introduce yourself first before you come and ask me who I am!'

Trying to backpedal Aaron changed his tone by a few degrees. 'Sorry, I'm Aaron. I was Mike's partner on and off for a few years.'

'Ah, you're that guy!' Abigail nearly choked on a giggle at Jasper's tone, and Harry pulled her to his side with an arm over her shoulders and put two fingers across her lips.

'Well, Abigail's just fine.' A deep chuckle. 'She and Harry just went upstairs for a little nap – well, that's what they said, anyway, but who knows? We had a pretty late night and we're all a bit jaded today. Sorry if I was abrupt, but I'm not used to being asked questions as if I'm a criminal.' He chuckled again. 'Not in my job!'

Another pause before Aaron asked, slightly hesitant now and disconcerted, 'So what's your job – if you don't mind telling me?'

'Sorry, can't tell you, it's classified, but let's say I work for a government agency in Wellington, not one you're likely to have heard of – well, most people haven't.'

Aaron thanked him and the front door closed,

but Jasper stayed where he was. Abigail and Harry waited silently, but as soon as Jasper returned to the kitchen they erupted in laughter.

'Right, he's gone – I kept an eye on him through the peephole.' Jasper looked pleased with himself. 'He stayed outside the door for a minute, trying to figure things out. He won't be able to find out anything about me, of course, officially I hardly exist – part of the job. And just in case you're wondering, James is the name I was given at birth, but I've been called Jasper since I was at school.'

'What an amazing performance!' Abigail wiped laughter tears from her cheeks. 'Hysterical! I can't believe how that nap innuendo came out so pat – did you think it up in advance?'

'Of course. I had to make sure he understood that trying to hook up with you was useless, so implying you two were having a little romantic interlude upstairs seemed perfect. I wish you could have seen his face – priceless doesn't even cover it.'

'I wish you could have seen Abigial's face – also priceless.' Harry shook his head at her. 'She very nearly ruined the whole thing. I practically had to gag her to stop her giggling.'

She held his gaze for a long moment, remembering the feel of his fingers on her lips, and he knew what she was thinking, she was sure of it. The blush she felt rising on her face made him smile, and once again she marvelled at the little things they understood about each other, as if both their intuitions were turned up high.

Shortly after an early lunch of pasta with pesto sauce, pieces of fried chorizo sausage and lots of grated parmesan, which Jasper said was the most satisfying winter meal he'd had in a long time, he got ready to leave. While they were sorting out notebooks and scribbled lists Abigail remembered something they hadn't even touched on. She put the screwed up sheets of paper in the rubbish bin and said urgently, 'But listen, how is this going to work in practical terms? You'll set Harry up with a documented background, and then what? What kind of ID or online identity will he need to access that documentation? He doesn't have an NHI number for health care or an Inland Revenue number. How will he prove who he is so he can access things?'

'Don't worry! I'll set up everything I can, it's all in my notes and then we'll take it step by step. I'll probably come down again, Harry, to show you everything and how it works.' Jasper fetched his bag from the hall and started putting his laptop and chargers into it. 'The other thing you need to discuss between you is how it's going to work if Harry sells the Brazil find. Earning money, when he has no history of ever having an income or paying tax. An adult suddenly appearing out of nowhere and earning huge sums of money. It will be a red flag for the tax department to look closely at him.'

'God, no! I didn't even think of that.' In Abigail's head threatening scenarios played out like little video clips; Harry arrested, Jasper's job once again in danger, herself in court.

'It's not urgent, is it?' Harry looked surprisingly calm, thought Abigail, considering the worrying ideas that now circled like sharks in her own head. 'We'll figure it out. There's no rush.'

Jasper left in a taxi after turning down Abigail's offer to drive him to the airport. 'Shit no! Don't get that new car out on this slipper stuff. I'd hate for you to get it smashed for no good reason. I'll be in touch!' He shook hands with Harry, hugged Abigail and then he was gone.

'What a great friend to have in an emergency like this,' said Harry and double-checked the front door was locked. 'And wasn't it perfect that you already had these blinds – I mean, when Aaron came, so he couldn't see who was coming to the door. It made the surprise even more effective.'

As if by mutual agreement, though not a word had been said, they didn't revert to any of the things they had worked on with Jasper. Abigail made them hot chocolate and went to the living room with her book, and Harry quietly continued working on his report. Outside the sky was dark gey and snow was falling again, though this time without the Antarctic wind blowing it sideways. The lantern outside the front door came on when the light level dropped and by mid-afternoon it felt like evening. Abigail pulled the curtains over the living room windows and in both bedrooms upstairs. Double glazing was wonderful, but today she felt a need to create a feeling of comfort; a cocoon to keep them warm and safe.

Harry came across her upstairs when she was pulling the curtains over the balcony doors and watched without comment, went to the bathroom and returned downstairs. On an impulse she got out of her jeans and sweatshirt and changed into the fleece so-called leisure suit, which she had bought a few years ago on a shopping expedition with Astrid, the one Mike had referred to as "your furry PJs" which had always made her laugh. 'Far too warm to sleep in, particularly next to you,' she used to say, 'but super cozy for a winter day at home.'

Back in the living room, she saw that Astrid had texted to say she was getting a sore throat, and someone at the library had real influenza, so she would stay away and not visit, then five minutes later she called.

'Oh God! Harry!' she exclaimed hoarsely. 'He won't have any antibodies to our bugs, will he? If he gets it he might die! You've got to get him vaccinated, Abigail – do it tomorrow. You'll just have to make something up, so they'll do it even though he's got no health ID or whatever it's called. Promise you will!'

'OK, I will, as soon as I figure out to explain who he is. Maybe an overseas tourist staying with me? I'll have to check if he's had any vaccinations in his timestream. It's all so complicated.'

'But the flu virus won't be the same in his timestream, so he'll need a new vaccination even if he's had one. I'll email you what I've dreamed up as a kind of back story.' Astrid's voice sounded more strained by the minute. 'And I've got some stuff I can drop off to you as a precaution, in case he gets ill, but my voice is giving out now and I've got to stop talking. I hope I didn't have this bug in my system when I was at your place!'

The email from Astrid an hour later. *"You could tell your doctor he's staying in your neighbour's house while they're away, and say you'll check with him if he's vaccinated already. Say you just asked in case he needs a vaccination. Say it's because you had him and some people for dinner two days ago and two of them have come down with something that's probably flu. Let me know how it goes, I feel really worried now. About Harry, I mean. I think I've got a slight fever, but nothing too bad, so hopefully it's just a sore throat and not the flu. As I said, I have an untouched box of antivirals that my doctor gave me last spring when he thought I might have shingles, but I never used them. It was just a weird rash. I'll drop them in your letterbox tomorrow just in case. Ax*

28

Harry was once again ensconced at far end of the kitchen table with both laptops open in front of him. Abigail studied him for a moment and decided against disturbing him, poured herself a glass of water and returned to the living room to call her doctor to find out how to get Harry vaccinated. But first she must decide if she was going to follow Astrid's script or something closer to what they had told Aaron. There were good reasons for both scenarios, but being consistent was safer than using different explanations in different contexts. After a few minutes thought she had an outline in her head and made the call.

'I'll put you through to the nurse,' said the receptionist. 'She'll sort it out, no need to talk to the doctor.'

'I've got a friend staying, he's been out of the country for some time, and we had some friends for dinner the other night,' said Abigail chattily to the nurse. 'And now I've just heard that one of those people is ill and thinks she might have the 'flu. So I feel concerned that Harry might have been exposed because he can't remember when he was vaccinated last for anything. His name is Harry Willims, and over the last few years he's spent a lot of time out of the country.'

She realised a bit of pleading might get her further than long explanations and added, 'I know he's not your patient, but he hasn't got a doctor down here yet, perhaps you can do it anyway seeing I'm a patient of yours? It's such an awkward situation.'

'Of course, just call and make an appointment with one of the nurses and tell the receptionist that we've already had a chat about this and to give him a ten minute appointment. He'll have to sit here for twenty minutes afterwards, so we know he's not going to have a bad reaction to the vaccine, but that's all.'

Abigail picked up her book, straightened the corner she had folded to mark her place and continued reading. Sometime later she slowly emerged from her intense involvement in the story and looked up, feeling dislocated from reality.

'You know what?' Harry was leaning against the doorframe looking at her across the room. 'When you're reading you're lost to the world, nothing registers. I've been standing here for a few minutes now - I cleared my throat twice and you didn't even look up. I even tried a little cough or two, but no reaction. Amazing!'

'It's a very good book,' said Abigail defensively. 'And apart from using me as a human experiment, do you need something, is there anything I can do for you?'

The moment she said it she knew how he might interpret her offer or pretend to interpret it. He gave her that look, the one she knew so well now. The look infused with desire and meaning, and as on previous occasions it made her blush, but this time she laughed when she felt her cheeks go pink. 'For God's sake! Are you giving me that look just so I'll blush?'

He grinned. 'I just love how receptive you are to what you call "that look". I'm not sure what the looks is, but it might be linked to what I'm thinking at the time,' he said innocently. 'Or maybe not. I came to ask if you want me to start making dinner. And to tell you I think I've found another of the ball lightning victims from the airport.'

This last piece of information was clearly added as an unimportant afterthought to tease her. She got to her feet in one fast move, ignored the book that fell to the floor and stared at him. 'Here?'

'No, no, not here - way up north. But let's go and sit in the kitchen and I'll show you. I have a feeling a glass of wine might be needed, so I poured it.' He looked at the book on the floor. 'Is that the book Astrid talked about?'

Abigail picked it up and put it on the arm of the chair. 'The Time Traveller's Wife – yes. Great story, very different and possibly one of the most absorbing books I've ever read. I'll let you read it when you've finished your report. Or is it finished already?'

'Not yet, but it will be soon,' he said over his shoulder and headed back to the kitchen. 'But let's talk about that later because what I've just found is far too interesting to wait.'

She sat down at the kitchen table and looked expectantly at his laptop. 'Show me right away or I'll expire of curiosity. I can't believe you found something concrete.'

He swung the laptop towards her and moved his chair closer. 'It's just like what happened to me – one major difference, but I'm sure I'm right. There are too many things that fit with my own experience. I've been looking here and there and tried to work out which search words work best, and today when I was having a little break, I made another search - and here it is.'

He clicked on a browser tab and said, 'See what you think.'

The article was dated 15 December 2021 and related an unusual event that had taken place in Whangarei. An elderly man in the suburb of Kamo had called the police and asked for assistance after opening his front door and finding a naked woman on the doorstep.

"Not only was I surprised she had no clothes on and no shoes," Mr Brooks told our reporter. "What was even more disturbing was that she said she didn't know where she was, she said she'd just before been at Auckland airport. I think the poor lady had some kind of breakdown, but the police came and said they'd take her to the hospital, so at least she's getting care. The cops came prepared with one of those silver blankets that look like foil and a kind of white overall, but I'd already sat her down wrapped up in an old dressing gown of my late wife's and given her a cup of tea. She had a shocking scar on her shoulder and right down her arm, like a dark brown, shiny mark. I've never seen one like it before – like she'd been in some ghastly accident, but not recent. It had healed long ago."

'Any more since?' asked Abigail and took a sip of wine, with her eyes still fixed on the screen in front of her. 'Did you follow up?'

'I haven't yet, just found it a few minutes before I came to get you. But I will, of course. Does sound a bit like me arriving on your doorstep, doesn't it?'

'It throws my original theory out the window,' said Abigail slowly, then paused to think and Harry waited silently. 'I had this picture in my mind of different timestreams existing in parallel but at different speeds – like you were in 2029 and got moved sideways in a straight line and landed here where it's 2026.' With her hands she sketched the timestreams in the air. 'So if someone was shifted to 2021, I would have thought they'd end up in a third timestream – one where a straight sideways shift coincided with 2021, not this one. It doesn't make sense.'

'I know. It doesn't make sense from how we imagined the timestream map that first morning, does it? But our ideas about time-and-space logic might be way off the mark. Perhaps things are far more complicated than that idea of timestreams we discussed. Maybe there are untold dimensions, maybe they loop back on themselves. How would we ever know?'

They looked at each other for a moment, both trying to come to grips with this new discovery and after what seemed like a couple of minutes of loaded silence, Abigail smiled. 'Oh, for God's sake!' she said, suddenly light-hearted. 'Who cares? We'll never know, and it doesn't matter. You can do some more research about that poor woman while I get some food ready, and then over dinner I'll tell you about Astrid's idea and her sore throat.'

'No, I'll set the table while you get dinner, and after dinner we can research the Kamo woman together. If I start it now, I'll get too involved and not want to stop – this is too interesting. If I saw a photo of her I might recognise her. It might be the woman I told you about, the one who was knocked to the ground further back from where I was – the one the ball lightning hit really hard before it got to me. But she wasn't the only one, of course.' He pushed the laptop to one side and got up. 'Perhaps we could try to contact that man Brooks, ask if he was kept informed about what eventually happened to her. And you must tell me what Astrid's idea is.'

'She's either got a really bad cold and a sore throat, or she might have influenza – not full on, because she was vaccinated in the autumn, of course. Someone at the library has it, and now she's worried about you.'

She crouched in front of the freezer compartment and moved things around while she talked. 'And she's quite right, of course – you won't have antibodies to our versions of colds and 'flu, so you need to be vaccinated. The clinic I go to will do it. All we need to do is make an appointment.'

She got up and put a bag of frozen potato wedges on the bench, followed by a packet of chicken bites. 'Fast food tonight – I'm over cooking for a couple of days, and you can save your efforts until I go back to work on Monday. And Covid! Good heavens, I just thought of that. Did you have a Covid epidemic in your timestream?'

'No, but I've read about it since I got here. I should be vaccinated against that too, I suppose. Let's get that done on Monday, please.'

. . .

Later that evening, when Abigail was in the garage with the charging cable for her new car in one hand and the manual in the other, there was a triumphant shout from the kitchen. She dropped the cable on the floor and hurried back still clutching the manual, and Harry started talking the moment she appeared.

'There's a long article in a magazine from 2022 about people who've experienced memory loss. This Kamo woman is mentioned right at the end as an example of someone who lost what they call her "life memory" or most of it and never regained it. They say sometimes people do, and it never comes back, but apparently they retain learned skills like reading and writing and how to tie their shoelaces.'

He looked expectantly at Abigail, who had sunk down on the chair beside him. 'She refused to be interviewed, and they don't name her - all they say is that she spent a couple of days in Whangarei hospital and was then moved to a neurological unit in Auckland.'

'And? I can tell there's a surprise waiting to jump out – it's written all over your face. What else did you find out?'

'She's still in touch with Mr Brooks! Would you believe it? They don't mention his name or the circumstances, but it's got to be her. It just says the authorities have never been able to establish who she is, or where she came from, or what had happened to her, but she's been supported since her hospital discharge by "the elderly man who first encountered her after her mysterious memory loss". We've got to find him!'

'Right, we need to map out a few things,' said Abigail slowly. 'I must make that vaccination appointment for you for Monday or Tuesday, and I must text Jasper and say we're sticking with Williams as a surname for you, because that's what I told the nurse. I should have talked to him first but never mind. And finding Mr Brooks, of course. And I'll start filtering in some gossip about you at work too, which will be useful if Frederick passes it on to Aaron. Let's call Jasper on What'sApp and work out the details of what I can say.'

29

To Abigail's relief Jasper seemed unfazed when she confessed what she had told the nurse about Harry. 'I don't think that's going to be a problem,' he said calmly. 'Put your phone on speaker and I'll tell you what I've done so far. Not much if you look at the situation as a whole, but it's a start – quite a bit of research.'

'It's on speaker already. I've decided we must both of us know everything, so we don't slip up some time in the future. So what have you managed so do so far?'

They heard things being moved around, a bit of clatter and then a muted curse. 'What's happening? Did we interrupt something?'

'I'm trying to locate the little notepad I wrote on at your place. I had it a minute ago and it's disappeared, so I'm moving every single thing on my desks and knocked my elbow in the process. Oh, here it is!'

'Desks?' Harry looked disbelieving. 'You have more than one?'

Jasper's laugh boomed out of the phone on the table and Abigail giggled. His laugh was the irresistible kind that made everyone who heard it smile or laugh. 'First I had one proper desk in what used to be my spare room, which is now my study. And then I needed more space for another couple of big screens and some new tech gear, so I put up a long, very wide shelf at desk height right along the wall where the bed used to be, so that's kind of like another two or three desks if you think of surface area. It's a great setup, but when I wheel my chair from one screen to the next I sometimes lose things. Or misplace them, because they're obviously still in this room somewhere. But I've got it now, the notepad, I mean.'

Abigail laughed outright. 'I can see it in my mind! Cables linked to mysterious black boxes, Post-it notes stuck to the walls, pens and tiny screwdrivers scattered and a bit of dust – total chaos, right? Not to mention external hard drives with strange writing on them in white marker pen.'

'Spot on! That's exactly how it is and how I like it. Anyway, I rushed to the office straight from the airport, spent two hours checking communication security for our embassies in three countries and found it was a false alarm. So I picked up a pizza and went home to do some research. Are you ready?"

'Yes!' said Abigail and Harry at the same moment

and Jasper laughed again. 'Fully synchronised already, very good! Now listen, Harry Williams is a good name if anyone tried to work out who you really are, quite common. But I think you should be David - you're just always called Harry. There are thousands of guys called David Williams all over the English speaking world, so it's a great camouflage name. And I think you'll have to be UK born after all, but we'll say you've lived here on and off since your early twenties. I'll set you up with permanent resident status and give you a fictitious birth date, something around the end of September, let's say the twenty-third. All with the aim of making you disappear into the masses.'

'Why September?' interrupted Abigail, who sensed Jasper was on a roll and would continue without input from them for several minutes. 'And why permanent resident status?'

'Most UK babies are born in September, always have been. Think about it, nine months after all the pre-Christmas parties and the New Year's parties and lots of alcohol, right? And permanent resident status is good provided it was issued at least ten years ago, because I can fudge an entry in the right place and get it to look right. Much harder to try to make it more recent, nearly impossible even for me. But here's something you'll have to consider seriously.' His voice faded and Abigail, said loudly, 'Stop Jasper, stop! You're walking away and you left the phone on the desk, didn't you? Please don't say anything important until you're back with that beer or we won't hear it!'

'You're really a witch, aren't you? How the hell did you know what I was doing?' Jasper's voice was back beside the phone.

She laughed. 'Jasper, my friend, I've known you long enough to know you always need another beer when you do a lot of talking. When we worked together I sometimes wondered if you filled your fancy stainless water bottle with beer every morning before you came to work. But never mind, you're back now and we can hear you.'

'And then there's a couple of other things – travel, driver's licence, and also the Companies Office registration. I'll start with travel. You said you didn't care if you never travelled, Harry. Did you mean it?'

Two perfectly parallel creases appeared between Harry's eyebrows and Abigail watched fascinated as over the next three or four seconds they gradually became less distinct and then vanished. 'Yeah, I do. I don't care if I can't travel. Being here and safe from anything that might happen at an airport or on a flight is really all I want now.'

'OK, that's good because the new software they're using for issuing passports in the UK is safer than Fort Knox. And I should know – my unit was asked to lend me to them to penetration test it, which is one of my much sought-after skills. So the only way to get you a passport would be to somehow get a fake one, which involves all kind of risks – not a good idea.'

For a brief moment Abigail's eyes met Harry's; he smiled, and she blushed, then he said. 'What the hell is penetration testing?'

Jasper chuckled. 'I know – it's always getting picked up on by people who aren't in my kind of job, but all it means is that someone, who knows all the hacker tricks, tries to break through firewalls and stuff. It's a way to check how safe something is. Which I'm very good at, being a hacker with huge experience, so our unit sometimes lends me to others.'

'OK, that makes sense, but what was the worry about the Companies Office?' asked Abigail. 'Are you setting up a company for him?'

'Brazil!' said Jasper and chuckled again. 'You might not have had time to think about it yet, but I think you should set up a company, Abby - register it with the Companies Office with yourself as the sole director, sell a few shares to me or Astrid or both to make it look genuine, and then the company sells the info about Brazil, and you don't have to officially do anything, Harry. Just keep on the right side of her, so she lets you spend the money.'

'Ah – well, that's up to Abigail, isn't it?' Harry sounded slightly hesitant. 'I mean, she might not want to get drawn into this thing. Not that I don't trust her, of course I do, but it would be such a weird thing for her to get involved in. How would she explain how she came across the knowledge in the first place?'

'We'll think of something – there's no rush, as you sometimes tell me, Harry.' Abigail surprised herself by not finding the idea at all strange or intimidating. 'I think it's a good idea and we'll work it out. Maybe information some friend left me in his will, or maybe I'm doing it for a friend who wants to stay anonymous, someone who's been there and knows how to write the report, but doesn't want anyone to know he found that site? Perhaps for political reasons?'

'Something like that – anything you can come up with that will convince some big mining conglomerate to take the proposal seriously and buy the info about the location. Harry, you're the expert, you'll have to decide how to go about it.'

They ended the call, turned on the dishwasher and went upstairs, but Abigail turned on the top step and went back down to check she had closed the door between the kitchen and the passage to the garage. When she returned Harry was still standing in the upstairs hall and the way he looked at her lit a flame of longing inside her.

'Come here,' he said and pulled her close, and with his mouth against her hair he murmured so quietly she could hardly make out the words, 'I love your mouth – it's luscious.' Then he held her away, kissed her forehead and let her go with a casual,

'Sleep well!' before he went into his room, leaving her standing there with her nerves tingling, aroused, and amused in equal parts.

She lay in bed with her eyes closed and re-lived the scene. The way his lips on her skin made a tight string of desire run down the centre of her body, the way those little touches over time had sensitised her to even the briefest and lightest touch now and not least, those quiet words. This drawn-out game he was playing was tantalising and seductive, a slow build-up, a promise of unknown delights. She lay there dreamily thinking back over all the little moves he had made and the way she could read his mind when he gave her that look. And she was playing a parallel game where she would wait and not take the next step, not give in to the temptation to turn this game of intermittent little flames into a blazing bonfire of lust and passion. I am so lucky, she whispered to herself and smiled in the dark, so lucky!

30

Mid-morning on Monday Jane wheeled a chair across to Abigail's desk. She had a mug of coffee in one hand and another resting on the seat of the chair.

'You're risking retribution of the worst kind!' Abigail and lifted the mug from the chair. 'What a mess that would have made if it tipped over and just think how angry Connor would have been when he comes back next week. That's his very personal chair, you know – he spent at least an hour readjusting it last time you'd borrowed it. He kept getting up and tweaking to the angles, huffing and puffing.'

'Such a fusspot!' said Jane callously. 'Served him right for calling me the town gossip. I should have put superglue on it, and we could have watched him struggle out of his pants to get up.'

The thought of chubby Connor stuck to his chair made Abigail laugh. 'Hot water will do it too –

you could have offered to pour it down the back of his pants. But seriously, what have you been up to while I was on leave?'

'Zilch, nothing, zero!' Jane made a face of disgust. 'Nothing in the least interesting happened here and not in my private life either. You know, Jim, the sexy guy I met at that wedding a couple of months ago? He's gone back to his partner, who'd kicked him out, so now I've got no one to go out with again, only girlfriends. How about you? Did you have a nice little break?'

Perfect, thought Abigail, here's my chance handed to me on a plate. 'I've got a friend of mine and Mike's staying for a while. He's thinking of living here permanently.' She gave Jane a sly smile and the reaction was exactly what he wanted.

'Aha, a man in the house? Goodlooking? Single? And how old? Tell me more!'

'Jane, stop! It's still a bit new and private.'

Jane just giggled. 'Well, what's he like? I saw that little smile when you mentioned him.'

'Totally gorgeous! And he's got a lovely personality – unlike any man I've known before. I always liked him when Mike and I used to go on skiing holidays with him, but I've got to know him in a different way now ...'

Jane smiled like the cat who got the cream. 'Aha! And he's unattached, I suppose, if he's come visiting on his own. How exciting! I hope I'll get to meet him.'

Out of the corner of her eye Abigail had noticed

Frederick, two desks away, turning his head slightly sideways at the sound of Jane's excited voice and she smiled inside. This could not have gone better if she had planned it, everything had fallen into place as if choreographed. The greatest gossip in the entire courthouse asking personal and inquisitive questions in a loud voice, and Frederick eavesdropping – there was no stopping it now.

And then it occurred to her that there was another layer to this news spreading operation and grabbed the opportunity. 'And listen to *this*!' she said making her voice just a pitch higher as if she was sharing a particularly good joke. 'Remember I told you about the guy I used to work with years ago in Wellington? The super code breaker? He came down for a couple of days too! Two lovely guys in the house at the same time, imagine that!'

'Lucky pig!' said Jane and rose to wheel Connor's chair back to his desk. 'You could share them out instead of hording them. Send one my way if your place gets cluttered. But good for you! Just what you need, I think.'

She picked up both mugs, and headed towards the lunchroom, and Frederick turned his head and glanced at Abigail for a moment before he faced his screen again.

To avoid anyone overhearing her, Abigail made the appointment for Harry's vaccination while taking a short and chilly walk during her lunchbreak. 'Yes, that's right,' she said to the receptionist. 'I talked to someone else about him a couple of days ago, I think it was Marion. His name is David Williams, but he's always called Harry and I think he was born in the UK. He'll need both the flu and Covid vaccinations, because he's been in South America for a while, and he hasn't kept up with his vaccinations.'

The blustery wind swept an icy draft across the back of her neck, so she turned her collar up and headed for the café just around the corner where she sometimes had lunch. Her sandwich could sit in the lunchroom fridge until tomorrow; the allure of the warm café and texting Harry without her fingers getting frozen was irresistible.

Just made appointment for your vaccinations for 6 tonight, it's their late night.

She had only just had time to take a sip of her coffee when her phone buzzed. 'Hi,' said Harry. 'Thanks for doing that – I suppose you'll take me there? Did you remember the details Jasper made up?'

'I just said you're David Wiliams, usually called Harry. I'll see you tonight - sorry, I must go, someone's approaching.'

Frederick was working his way towards her through the crowded café. 'Do you mind sharing your table?' he asked innocently. 'There aren't any free ones – I hope you don't mind.'

'Of course I don't mind. Is this your favourite lunch place too?'

'It's everyone's favourite place,' he said and glanced around. 'I can see at least half a dozen people from the court, probably more.'

Their orders were delivered nearly at the same time, a club sandwich for Abigail and a ham and cheese toastie for Frederick. 'I hope you won't feel I deliberately eavesdropped on you and Jane this morning,' he said casually after taking a bite. 'I couldn't help hearing Jane's voice – you can hear her all over the office when she gets excited. So you have a new man in your life, do you?'

She looked steadily at him for a long moment before she replied, as if she was evaluating him, assessing if she should tell him or not, but what she was really doing was buying time to mentally scroll through ideas about how to use this opportunity.

'I suppose you could say that, yes. One of those things that happen – someone you've known for years and always got on really well with, and then it changes into something else. I'm very lucky because I really don't like living on my own, even with a good home security system.'

Frederick still tried to make out he was only casually interested and said, 'Oh, I quite understand – not when you're used to company and then suddenly find yourself living alone.'

Abigail took a sip of her coffee and studied him over the rim of the cup. He was quite successfully appearing only vaguely interested, and not too inquisitive, but she felt sure he was more alert than that.

'But I don't think you *do* understand,' she said seriously. 'It's hard for a man to completely grasp how vulnerable a woman feels sometimes. How being on your own makes you feel anyone can try to take advantage, or worse. But Mike got the security system upgraded to a whole new level with face recognition and stuff, just amazing.' A little lie wouldn't come amiss, she thought and smiled innocently across the table. 'Imagine! I can even program in a particular make and model of car and get an alert on my phone if one stops outside – at night, say. Like someone sitting out there looking at the house.'

Now Frederick's eyes were riveted on her face, and his hand stirring his coffee had stopped mid-movement. She continued innocently, 'It's been useful already more than once. I'm not saying I'm being stalked, but if someone's too persistent it's good to be aware. And I keep video clips of those events in case I need to use them some time in the future. My lawyer said they'd be vital if I need to take out a restraining order.'

I can see his mind working at full speed, she thought and tried to keep her expression neutral. I bet he's got no idea I know he and Aaron are mates. He never saw me in the restaurant, he and Aaron both had their backs half towards me, and they would have left through the bar door that leads to the side street. I don't think I've ever seen that connecting staff door to the bar left open before. Perhaps he knows Aaron's been watching the house, perhaps this information will be texted to Aaron straight after we part. What a useful day this has been.

Driving home she thought of potential pitfalls at the clinic and realised how odd it might look that she paid for Harry's vaccinations. Wouldn't any adult simply pull a card out and pay for themselves? As soon as she was inside the house, she got her ATM card out and handed it to Harry.

'Did you have these in your world, cards you swipe though a slot on little machine to pay? I want you to know how to pay with it at the doctor's clinic. It would look weird if I paid for you.'

He took card and turned it over in his hands. 'Ours didn't look like this, though. What's the little silver square? Is it just a decoration?'

She poured herself a glass of water, noted that something was cooking in the over and sat down at the table. 'It shows there's a computer chip inside the card so you can swipe it over a terminal instead of inserting it in the slot. If you swipe it you don't have to enter your personal PIN, but if the expense is greater than $80 swiping doesn't work.'

'So if it costs more I'll have to enter the PIN? How many digits?'

'Four – 1812.'

He sat down, still with the card in his hand. 'What's the significance?'

'The 1812 Overture is one of my favourite

pieces of music to see performed live. But listen, let's go through exactly how it works, so you don't fumble. I must get you a card on my account, maybe a debit card would be perfect so you can use it on the internet and in shops.'

Taking Harry to get his vaccinations ramped up their little game to new level. Not that Abigail had planned it, but for the third time that day a perfect opportunity presented itself. When the nurse asked Harry to follow her to a treatment room, Abigail got to her feet and seeing the surprised look on the nurse's face she said coolly with a little smile in Harry's direction, 'He's terrified of needles. He just told me on the way here, so I'll divert his attention when you do the needle sticks.'

The look Harry gave her behind the back of the nurse was a mix of held back laughter and something else she couldn't quite define, possibly a silent promise of retribution. She gave him a bland smile in return and proceeded to stand beside him during the brief procedure, with her hand resting on his shoulder. He looked at her with narrowed his eyes and she said comfortingly, 'It only hurts if you watch, it's a scientific fact.'

The woodment they were in the car, he turned to her and said with an expression of relish, 'You just wait, my girl! I'll not forget that comment about how I'm scared of needles! You've ruined my manly reputation, that nurse thinks I'm a coward.'

She laughed. 'Don't be silly – it's a fact that far more men than women are frightened of needles, nothing to be ashamed of. I just wanted to be in there with you in case she asked something and tripped you up.'

'Yeah, right – you're a devious little handful, you are. As I said, I'll not forget it.'

31

Abigail spent considerable time both in quiet moments at work and lying awake in bed working out a plan for how to not only find Mr Brooks, but how to remain anonymous when she contacted him, which seemed important. It was only one morning when she heard a colleague mention his so-called secondary email address that she found the answer to at least the main problem.

'I set it up years ago,' he said when someone asked him what it was for. 'You know, just to have one when you buy stuff online and they ask for your email. Having a second address means my main email account doesn't get clogged up with spam or special offers or whatever. I only use it for online shopping.'

Abigail took no part in the ensuing conversation, because now that she knew how to safely contact Mr Brooks while still retaining her privacy, she couldn't resist the temptation to there and then start composing the email she would send him. She thought of and rejected half a dozen ideas before she hit on what seemed the perfect plan.

That evening they had *pasta verde* with grated parmesan and a glass of red wine, all set out ready by Harry when she arrived home late, after driving the new car on very icy streets for the first time.

'Imagine,' she said happily over dinner, 'my new car reacts nearly before it goes into a little slide on the ice. It's amazing, it knows just what to do and does it a second of two quicker than I would. I had no idea it could do that.' She laughed at herself. 'When all else fails, read the manual, as they say. God knows what else it might be able to do that I haven't discovered yet. And this meal was lovely, it's one of favourite dishes, real comfort food.'

'I know. You told me one night just after I arrived, so I looked it up on the internet. And so lucky that you grow parsley and things in those pots on the windowsill. But tell me what you're going to say to Mr Brooks when you email him – if he has an email account.'

She twirled the stem of her wineglass between her fingers and considered her various ideas and how many of them had potential pitfalls. 'I've rejected several ideas because there might be some little thing that would lead him to ask tricky questions.'

She put the wineglass down and ticked them off

on her fingers. 'I must avoid any mention of a different year from this one, and I mustn't say "I know", if he says she came from 2029 or something about a different world, and I can't tell him at the start what my imaginary friend looked like or her age. I have to quote both articles because otherwise I can't explain how I know his name, and I won't mention my friend's name. I'll have to act like I'm a bit mentally disorganised – quite a list! I'm not sure how to avoid some of those things, but I'm working on it.' She thought back to her planning in the night. 'Oh yes, and I'll not mention of you at all, of course, it's all about my imaginary friend. But the first thing we must do is find the man and how to contact him.'

'I've done that,' said Harry surprisingly and laughed at her outraged expression.

'What!? And you didn't tell me the moment I walked in the door!'

'I was keeping it as a surprise for you, and we had so much else to talk about I forgot. He's on Facebook, but he's never posts anything. Maybe you can send him one of those private messages you told me about. Check it out after dessert.'

She couldn't help laughing. 'Dessert? You're turning into a kitchen maestro, Harry! God, I'm so glad you crash landed on my front lawn, best thing that ever happened to me.'

Instead of replying he walked up behind her chair and leaned forward, put his hands on her shoulders and kissed the top of her head before he went to fridge. 'Here you are, something I learned on the internet today. It's called apple snow.'

He placed a small bowl full of what really looked like snow, white and fluffy, in front of her and for a brief moment she thought he was teasing, maybe it was real snow. But after one mouthful of delicious frothy apple, slightly acidic, but sweet, she exclaimed in surprise. 'This is gorgeous! I never heard of it before. What's in it? Apples put through the blender, sugar and maybe a bit lemon juice? Gelatine?'

'Exactly! I've been watching those apples in the fruit bowl we never seem to get around to eating, so I told Google to find me very simple apple recipes with few ingredients, and this was one we had all the ingredients for. There's a lot more of it in the fridge. Apparently you need the lemon juice to stop the apple mush turning brown which I didn't know. Acidic lemon juice as a food anti-oxidant.'

She took another mouthful and looked seriously at him, wanting him to realise she truly meant it, 'You are amazing – like a present from the sky. Thank you!'

'The thank-you goes both ways, you know. There can't be there another person in the universe who'd react as you did when you opened the door that night. And let's not mention all you've done for me since, not just to keep me safe. Maybe I should have said, all you do to me.' He gave her that look of his and watched her face go pink then laughed. 'My God, that's amazing, you read my mind again'

'Stop it! I can't eat with that kind of thing going on.' Abigail took another mouthful of chilled apple snow to distract herself. 'And listen, I can't contact Mr Brooks with a Facebook private message. Then he'd know who I am, and I'm not prepared to let him discover that. I'm going to set up another email account, and I'll call myself Abby. If he's not got an email account I'll have to find some other way to contact him.'

But when she found him on Facebook she laughed. 'Look at this! He's got no privacy settings at all, look here.' She showed Harry where to look for his personal details. 'Here's his phone number and his email address – and his birth date. Goodness, he's very old, I hope he's still alive. I bet someone said he should have a Facebook account and being old school and not used to taking online precautions, he simply entered everything they asked for. So it's easy to get in touch with him. I'll compose an email message, and you can check it, and then I'll set up that second email account.'

Dear Mr Brooks,

You don't know me, but I found your email address on Facebook. I found an old article from 2021 on the internet about a woman who came to your door with no knowledge of where she was. Then I found the article in

Women's Review about how she's still in touch with you. A dear friend of mine left the South Island to move to Kaitaia that year and then all communication stopped, and I have been unable to find a way of contacting her since. May I call you? Just so I can check if the woman you found might be her?

Kind regards, Abby

'Perfect,' said Harry after reading the draft message she had composed in a Word document. 'Not too much information, and I think the tone of it is good, just right to appeal to someone as old as he looks to be.'

'Oh, good! I'll set up the email account now and send him the message, and then we'll see – provided he's alive and checks his emails, or course. Maybe he only turns his computer on once a week or something.'

Much to her surprise the reply from Mr Brooks pinged into her new account only an hour later.

Dear Abby,

I would like to talk to you, but I won't mention anything about this to the lady who turned up at my door, as she gets agitated these days if anyone tries to find out more or tries to force her memory. And I wouldn't like to raise her hopes that you know who she is. She has settled very well, and I don't want to upset her or make her worry. We never discuss it now. Please feel free to phone me so we can talk. Tomorrow night would be good because she's going out to dinner at half past six. Call after seven, so I have time to watch the news first.

    Kind regards, Albert Brooks

32

The previous evening Abigail had felt obliged to make Harry understand why she didn't want him to take any part in her talk with Mr Brooks. She was acutely aware of how dangerous it might be if Harry took part in the exchange and was tempted to let on too much about his own story; even an unguarded exclamation might do it. If the naked lady was not from the airport incident, but he accidentally revealed his own background, there was no way of predicting what might happen next.

'It would be so easy to say just one thing that would put you in danger,' she concluded. 'We just can't take the risk.'

'What do you mean by danger? You mean he might report me or something? Or make a news item out of it.'

'What if he got really intrigued and started asking for details and got the drift of what happened to you and then told someone? You saw how cagey he was in the email, he didn't even mention her name or what she told him when she turned up or anything. So he's protecting her, but your details might be too tempting.'

'So you mean to go no further than what you put in your email, even if something really interesting crops up?'

Abigail thought carefully about how to put this to avoid insulting Harry but still keep him safe. 'Listen,' she said seriously after a couple of moments. 'My idea is that I don't mention you, so Mr Brooks never gets to know there's another time-slip victim here, even if his lady is one. I just continue along the lines of what I put in the email, that I'm wondering if she's my long lost friend and how I don't want to upset the woman he's been helping in case she isn't my friend. I made up that vague story so we could keep this centred on something harmless.'

She tried to pull her thoughts into order. 'I think I should just talk about how she arrived and ask if he has a photo of her. He only seems to have a landline, there was no mention of a cell phone number on Facebook, so I don't know how that would work – I'm reluctant to give him my address to mail a photo to me. The whole point of using that second email account I set up is to keep you safe and not risk the background Jasper is creating for you.'

Harry considered for a minute, his gaze in the

middle distance without focus like always when he was pondering a tricky question. Abigail waited patiently and when he replied she heaved an internal sigh of relief. 'OK, you're right. I'll stay quiet however intriguing this gets, but I might pass you a note if I think of something.'

At quarter past seven she put the phone on the table between them and dialled Mr Brooks' number, then turned both the recording and the speaker functions on as soon as he answered.

'Hi, Mr Brooks, it's Abby. Thanks for agreeing to talk to me.'

'Good evening, Abby – and just Bert will do, no need to be formal. What can I tell you that might help? If your friend disappeared several years ago, wouldn't her family have reported her missing by now? Have they still heard nothing?'

This was a question Abigail had anticipated, one of many, and she said calmly, 'That's the trouble, she had no family here in New Zealand, and I only got hold of her brother in England late last year, and he didn't seem worried. Their parents are dead, and he never got on with his sister – imagine, he said he hadn't noticed he hadn't heard from her for years! But he promised to tell me if she contacts him. Was there anything your woman could tell you about herself? Any details that might help me decide if it could be my friend.'

Bert cleared his throat, then coughed and they heard a rustle. 'I've got three pages the police let me have about things she said to them, both here and later. I only got given these because the neurology doctors in Auckland said I should have them when they heard she was going to come and live with me after she was discharged. They thought I should have the facts in case I could winkle out some more, and so I could remind her of what she said at the beginning in case that triggered her memory.'

'That was a good idea!' said Abigail encouragingly. 'And has it helped in any way?'

'Just a little,' said Bert and coughed. 'Sorry, I've got a cold. Now I'm so old I seem to catch infections very easily. Did I tell you I'm eighty-nine? But never mind that. I've written a few things by hand on these pages the cops gave me, things that have come up since, so I won't forget them. Shall I read them out?'

'Oh, please do! I'd love to hear what you've discovered. There was so little in that second article.'

'That's because I warned them. They tried, but I said I'd get my lawyer onto them if they didn't respect her privacy. This is how it was - when I opened the door she said, 'I don't know where I am.' She looked absolutely terrified. So I asked her to come in, didn't want people staring at the poor naked thing. Once I got her into my late wife's dressing gown I sat her down with a cup of tea and a biscuit at my kitchen table and called the cops. They talked to her quite a bit when they came, particularly the woman cop. She was very good with her, very gentle.' He had a coughing fit and

Abigail waited in silence. 'All she knew was that she had been at the airport in Auckland with her boyfriend, waiting to get on a plane to Fiji for a two week holiday. She had no idea how she got to be on my doorstep, stark naked and without any possessions, couldn't remember her name or address. Not a thing! She still doesn't, but we never talk about it now.'

'It's very strange,' said Abigail, 'but maybe someone had abducted her? Did they consider that?'

'Oh, yes,' said Bert. 'That was one of the first things they thought of, maybe she'd been abducted and drugged or something. Because turning up like that with no clothes – it seemed like she might have run off from someone who'd held her captive. And that huge scar over her shoulder and down her arm, all brown and shiny, I've never seen anything like it, must have been a terrible injury.'

'It's very confusing,' said Abigail slowly. 'A real mystery. Could she give a date of when she was meant to take that flight to Fiji? Couldn't they check security cameras at the airport if they knew when to look?'

Bert seemed to have forgotten they were only trying to establish if the naked lady was Abigial's friend and was happy to continue discussing his surprise visitor. 'They did that when she mentioned the airport, but there was no sign of her there. She only knew those few things, still knows no more today than she did back then. They even checked for a passenger who hadn't got on a flight to Fiji –

several weeks back, but nothing came of it. Oh, I forgot, here it is on the next page - once she'd calmed down a bit she said she's a trained nurse, her boyfriend's name is Barton, and she thinks her first name began with the letter K, but she wasn't sure, and she still isn't. Between us we decided Kate was a good name, so that's what she goes by now, and she'd borrowed my surname, seeing she didn't have one.'

Abigail took in Harry's shocked expression, and she knew why; this was the most incredible coincidence. 'How old do you think she is – or was when she first arrived?'

Bert chuckled wheezily. 'Anyone under fifty looks young to me these days, but the cops and the doctors agreed she was probably about thirty-five then. Very pretty, with thick dark brown hair and big brown eyes. She's still pretty, of course, and she lives here in the granny flat at the back of my house. We have meals together a couple of times a week. It's nice for me, like having a niece or a daughter. Which I never had.'

'What does she do? Does she work?'

He chuckled again. 'Oh yes, she's a hard worker. She's had a job at the same place nearly since she came back from the hospital in Auckland, at a pharmacy in town. She's going out with one of the men who does people's gardens, the one who mows my lawn, Jonathan. Very nice chap! They go camping and kayaking together.'

And then he suddenly exclaimed, 'Oh, wait a

minute! I forgot to say, when she turned up she thought the year 2029! It was the oddest thing, she really did, she insisted and got very agitated and cried when the cops said no, it was 2021. They asked her if she knew the date and the year – apparently they do when people have strokes and lose their memories, or whatever.'

With a huge effort Abigail collected her thoughts and tried to sound composed. 'Well, thank you very much, Bert! It's kind of you to talk to me, but it's definitely not my friend Alison. She was closer to fifty when she left here, and she had blue eyes. I should have asked you first about this woman's looks, but I got so interested in what you had to tell me that I forgot.'

'That's fine Abby – it was nice to have a chat. I hope you find out what happened to your friend.'

Abigail ended the call and looked carefully at Harry, who was looking strained. 'Shit!' he said on a muted groan. 'I don't believe it! This is the most incredible thing, isn't it? It's Katrina!'

'I thought she must be when you reacted to strongly – obviously the description was spot on? Let's sit down in the living room and have a glass of Bayley's or maybe cognac is called for.'

She got up without waiting to see how he reacted, acutely aware of how shocked he was and that he might want to be alone to think it over. But by the time she had poured their drinks and turned from the sideboard he was in his usual armchair, looking slightly overwhelmed, but in control. She handed him the glass and sat down.

'I'd like to try to understand this, if you don't mind talking about it.' He nodded but said nothing. 'So when the ball lightning hit you, you had just come back from Brazil, and you were waiting for an internal flight at Auckland airport. And on the same day Katrina was at Auckland airport heading for Fiji with her boyfriend Barton! But why was she in Auckland? Why didn't they fly from the South Island? It's a massive coincidence, isn't it – both the day and the place? Did she know when you were due to return?'

He was silent for so long she got seriously worried, then finally he started talking, hesitantly at first. 'This is what I think must have happened – it's the only explanation that fits the facts. She must have figured out that I had overheard part of her chat with Jenny. Maybe she heard the front door close again when I went for my little walk, or she felt the air movement through the house? And if she then looked out at the street she would have seen me walking away.'

He thought for a moment. 'I can't think of any other way she could have known that I heard what she said. I know I wasn't very friendly those last couple of days before I left for Brazil, so that probably confirmed it in her mind.'

'And she didn't know when you were due to return from Brazil?'

'No, I never told her. It was an open-ended ticket when I left, and I had no contact with her while I was away, even my office didn't know. I think she must have decided to leave me while I was in Brazil, and she and Barton were celebrating with a trip to Fiji. And in my world there's only one international airport and that's Auckland. People don't travel half as much as they seem to do here, nowhere near it.'

They sat in silence sipping their drinks until Harry said, suddenly decisive. 'Your strategy of not emailing Bert from your usual account and calling yourself Abby was a great idea. It protects your identity, and that degree of separation will keep you out of any follow-up. Not that it seems likely there'll be any. I realise I'm not married to Katrina in this timestream, but I want you to be anonymous in all this.'

'I didn't do it to protect myself,' said Abigail quietly. 'I did it for you. I worried something would reveal your story, something you might have said to Bert, anything at all. And I couldn't let that happen, so I took precautions.'

He got up and reached for her hand. 'Could you stand up, please? I'm so lucky to have you in my life now, I can't even tell you how good it feels.'

Held tight against his chest with her arms around his back Abigail stood silently revelling in the feeling it gave her to stand like this. They remained there for a long time, close together without moving or speaking, and this time there was no flash of sexual attraction, just comfort and calm. Before they stepped apart Harry whispered a couple of words into her hair, so silently that they were nearly inaudible. 'You're mine,' he breathed, and she knew she was not meant to have heard and made no response.

33

When Jasper called after dinner on Thursday night Abigail decided to invite him to come for another couple of days. There were things she hoped Harry would agree to tell him, but not over the phone. It would be much better doing it face to face in a relaxed setting.

'I know you want to tell us about what you've set up for Harry, so how about I shout you another trip down here for the weekend? We've got things to tell you too, and having time to do it leisurely over dinner is such a nice thing, isn't it? And Astrid could be here too, so we don't have to repeat things. What do you think?'

'Fine with me,' said Jasper. 'The love affair's gone down the tube in a woosh of regret and lame excuses – the excuses are his, not mine, so another weekend down there would be nice. I presume you've found out something interesting?'

'Very intriguing,' said Harry who was listening

to the conversation with Abigail's phone on speaker as usual. 'And you've got things to tell us?'

'Yep, it's all done, I've just got to tell you how to use it. And most importantly, what not to do. I've made some notes for you about that side of things. I'll buy a ticket for Saturday morning, and book myself in at the same hotel as last time, very nice place.'

'No, I'm paying, Jasper. Please, let not argue about it. Mike's life insurance payout is sitting in a high interest bearing account and earning money faster than I can use it. '

The idea that Jasper would be out of pocket was unacceptable. He owed her a favour, yes, but it was his skills that provided the favour. Costing him money was a different thing altogether. 'I'm serious, Jasper, so let's not debate it! You've rescued us in this weird situation, and we owe you big time.'

When they ended the call a few minutes later Abigail texted Astrid and invited her for dinner on Saturday. 'Some interesting news,' she wrote cautiously, 'and Jasper will be here, so come along any time after mid-afternoon.'

'Why mid-afternoon?' asked Harry when she told him. 'Any particular reason?'

'We're going to the supermarket now,' said Abigail coolly without responding and pulled his pad towards her. 'Let's decide what to have for dinner and lunch in the weekend, and we'll go now because after eight the place is probably empty.'

'We? Am I going shopping? Wow!' Harry

laughed. 'I've been waiting for you to let me out for real, not just for a drive in the car. I can't wait to see what your supermarket's like. Anything else open this late?'

'Fast-food places are, and restaurants and bars and things, but not most shops – oh, wait a moment, Kmart and all those mega sized shops are all open till ten or eleven, I think. Let's go on a shopping expedition!'

'Amazing!' was Harry's verdict when they entered Kmart. 'What a huge place – I've never seen anything like it. Let's just walk around for a while. I can't buy anything, but it's interesting to check things out.'

'Oh God, I'm sorry!' Abigail stopped and looked apologetically at him. 'You *do* have money now and a card for your own use – I just hadn't given it to you yet. It was in the mail yesterday and I set up the PIN for it in my lunch break today. It's a debit card so you can use it as a credit card online or as an ATM card in a shop - here.'

She fished around in her shoulder bag and handed him a card. 'It's got my name on it, but it links to an account that I set up for you, a sub-account that hangs off my main spending account. I've put an automatic transfer in place for the first of every month, but we'll have to see if it's enough – time will tell. Please don't try to pay for a car without warning me first!'

Harry, who has stopped when she handed him the card, simply stared at her. 'You're mad!' he said sounding nearly angry. 'You can't do this! It's too much, miles too much.'

Abigail had expected this exact reaction and had spent some time deciding on the best way of dealing with it, so she said cheerfully, 'Get used to it! This is your new normal for the time being. Don't forget the insurance policy and all that money just sitting there earning interest. It's unearned wealth, I've done nothing to deserve it, and we'll just regard it as a useful joint thing. So because you can't have a bank account, or not until Jasper tells us if it's possible without whatever ID the banks demand, this is how we do it. And then you sell that mining info and get millions for it, and we'll þe even better off.'

Harry shook his head, still set to firmly turn her offer down, and she could see he was about to hand the card back. On an impulse she moved right up close, reached up with a hand on his shoulder and put her lips on his. His indrawn breath of surprise was thrilling, and she felt powerful, as if she could do anything. She ran the tip of her tongue slowly along his bottom lip and gave it a light nip with her teeth before she stepped back.

'Please?' she said softly, as if she was asking a favour. His reaction had felt like a little electric shock and in her head she triumphed, 'One – nil to me!'

He followed her single step back with one

towards her, leaned in close and said very quietly, 'You just wait, my girl!'

They stayed there, their bodies nearly touching, looking into each other's eyes, oblivious of other shoppers walking past and around them. Then his eyes moved to her mouth, and she felt his desire like a hot touch on her skin. 'Thank you!' he said after what seemed like an eternity and took a step to one side. 'Let's go.'

They left Kmart more than an hour later with four paper carrier bags and headed for the supermarket. 'God, look at the time!' Harry chuckled. 'Doesn't time fly when you're having fun! Will the supermarket be open still? It's nearly ten now.'

'The one I go to doesn't close until eleven, I think, or even midnight. I'll try to think if there's anything else we need apart from what we put on the list. I have a feeling you'll be impulse shopping there too, so we'd better have one of us concentrating.'

'That was such fun! We didn't have anything like that Kmart shop in my world – nowhere near it, and no shops were open after six or so. I can't wait to see what the supermarket is like.'

At quarter past eleven Abigail drove into the garage and turned to Harry. 'Here's the rule from now on. Either you go shopping on your own and do whatever you want to do, or we go together and take an oath to stick to the list. I have *never ever* come home with more impulse bought items than those on the list.' Then she grinned at Harry's expression of surprise at her tone. 'Only kidding – that *was* fun! Let's unpack this car, it's sagging under the weight.'

34

In bed that night Abigail lay quietly thinking of the little minimal kiss in Kmart and how his surprise and instant physical reaction made her long to take it one step further. If they hadn't been standing in the middle of a shop she might have finally given in to temptation and taken the next step, after which there would be no stopping or pulling away. Two staff members had been watching their little performance, something she only realised after Harry stepped away, but she managed to ignore them and pretend she hadn't noticed.

But now something alerted her even though the house was quiet and there was no sound from Harry's room. It was like a change in air pressure, as if a door had opened and air from outside changed the atmosphere inside. She sat up in her bed and listened carefully before she got up and tiptoed out into the hall, but as soon as she set foot there she knew it wasn't an open door or window, it was Harry. His door was very nearly shut and there was no light on in his room. She knew with total certainty that something was wrong. Intense anxiety propelled her forward and as soon as she was inside his bedroom the feeling grew stronger, painfully so, as if something was squeezing her tight. Harry was lying on his back, perfectly still with his arms by his sides. Enough diffuse light from the streetlights came through his window, where the curtains were pulled apart, and she saw him clearly. He's not breathing, she thought, and fell to her knees beside the bed, put a hand on his chest and stifled a sob of panic.

'Oh, no!' her voice cracked. 'Oh, please don't do this to me - please!' She flung an arm across his chest and rested her forehead against his ribcage, overcome by an intense feeling of loss. Then a hand came to rest on her head and Harry said, 'Abigail? What's the matter, darling? Did you have a nightmare again?'

All she could do was cry. The transition from thinking he had died to hearing his voice sounding perfectly normal was too much, she simply couldn't snap out of the feeling that had gripped her when she thought he had died.

Harry sat up, took a firm grip on her upper arms and half lifted, half dragged her higher and tilted her sideways to lie beside him. And still she sobbed, unable to stop, as if she were frozen in that moment of shock. He said nothing, just pulled her close, wrapped both arms around her and rocked her gently, until her sobs died away, and she said in a shaky voice, 'I thought you were dead. I felt something from my room – and then you were so still and …'

'And what?'

'I couldn't see your chest moving, and I panicked.'

'What did you feel from your room? Did you hear something?'

She realised that her face was against his neck and her lips moved against his skin when she spoke, an intimate feeling as potent as a kiss. 'I was already awake, just lying in bed and then it felt as if the air pressure in the house changed. like it does when you suddenly open an outside door, so I got up.'

'I think you must have sensed my nightmare – it was about you, about us. I was caught in a terrifying dream where I was back in my previous life. In the dream I knew I had been here, I remembered everything, but I couldn't get back to you and I was frantic. One of those awful frustrating dreams were everything goes wrong, and you keep trying but you never get anywhere and just go around in circles. But I'm not dead, I'm very much alive.' He gave snort of laughter and held her closer still. 'Can't you feel how alive I am?'

He moved slightly and she realised he was not

only very alive, but he was also impressively aroused. She laughed quietly, suddenly calm again, and reached down to touch him and the slowly smouldering fuse of mutual attraction finally reached the dynamite, and the explosion blasted coherent thought sky high.

In the morning Abigail woke up and knew without opening her eyes that she was in Harry's room. She was tucked in with the quilt up over her shoulders and without turning she could feel that Harry wasn't behind her in the bed. She slitted her eyes open, hoping it wasn't morning yet, but it must be. Early winter morning and still dark outside, and the whole scene in the room had changed from the nighttime drama and passion. Now the curtains were pulled across the window, the bedside lights were on, and Harry appeared in the doorway with a tray and a look of total concentration on his face.

'Oh good, you're awake! Would you please sit up and sit *very* still.' He walked around the bed, slid carefully onto the bed, still with the tray held perfectly horizontally and turned slightly to put it between them. 'Are you warm enough?'

The smile alerted her, and she realised she was naked, burst out laughing and looked around. 'I don't know where I put my PJs last night.'

'You didn't – I did. Here's the top half.' Harry reached behind him, still moving slowly and plucked her top from the bedhead. 'Careful how you move when you put it on! I over-filled the mugs. I should have used that thermos you have in the pantry, but I didn't think of it until I was halfway up the stairs.'

She studied the tray and smiled. 'My God, you're such a great looker-after! I haven't had breakfast in bed since I was seven or eight and in bed with tonsillitis.'

Half an hour later, with coffee no long in danger of spilling and the toast eaten, she turned to look closely at him. 'Why were you sleeping like that last night? Flat on your back with your arms down along your sides. Suck a weird posture – or at least it seems weird to me.'

'I often sleep on my back, but I'm surprised I wasn't snoring – then you'd have known right away I wasn't dead. No, wait, I take that back! Then you'd have just gone back to your room and none of this sexy stuff would have happened.' He put his hand on her thigh and smiled. 'And I must say you looked delicious earlier with your curls all over the place and nothing on. Good enough to eat!'

'You are stupendously good at this!' said Abigail an hour later after long, slow sex that at one stage had her gasping in ecstasy. 'You're my best present ever. Can I please unwrap you every night?'

They were lying facing each other with their noses nearly touching. 'I wrote a poem about you – well, about us, I suppose.'

'Nobody's ever written a poem about me before.'

His hand on her hip tightened its grip and she knew he was touched. 'Will you read it out to me?'

Shel sat up and concentrated, tried it out in her head and decided she could remember it, then she recited her poem.

'The Now is known, the Then might be,
    The Why is lost, the Where is too.
    But out of What? springs hope anew,
    For me at least, maybe for you.'

Then her tone changed, and she added quickly, 'But you've got to see it written down because all those words, now, then, why, where and what – they're all written with the first letter in upper case. I think it makes the meaning far clearer, if you see it.'

'I heard those upper case letters, and I love the poem. Are you going to embroider it on a cushion so we can have it on the sofa?'

'What a hideous idea! And I can't embroider to save my life – don't be silly. I wrote it when I was awake one of the first nights you were here. I kind of wrote it in my mind, but I remembered in the morning and typed it into the Notes app on my phone.'

'You're a treasure – no doubt about it!'

'One thing, though, and I'm serious now,' said Abigail. 'You know that look - the one you do to make me blush? Please don't do it when anyone else is around, because now I'll have this experience of stupendous sex with you popping into my head when you look at me like that, and I'll turn scarlet not just pink. So embarrassing!'

'I'll save that look for my private enjoyment,' said Harry. 'Just when I can't resist.'

When Abigail heard Jasper's taxi stop outside just after midday on Saturday, she turned to Harry before she went to open the door, still worried about his decision to tell all. 'Are you quite sure you want to tell him about Katrina and not regret it later? It's so personal and when you told me you seemed so angry with yourself for falling for her tricks – it's not easy to talk about things like that. Can you cope with all the questions?'

'Quite sure,' said Harry calmly. 'I've thought about it these last couple of days since you first mentioned it, but let's do it later when Astrid's here. I think they need to know, and if I don't tell them the back story we can't tell them about Mr Brooks. It was good that you recorded that phone conversation, so we don't have to try to remember and re-phrase everything he said.'

After hugs and greetings Jasper put his large

canvas satchel on one of the chairs by the kitchen table and talked as he lifted things out. 'I've brought my regular laptop, and the one that doesn't have wifi capability that I never connect to the internet, a couple of hard drives and some notes I printed out. I couldn't remember if you have a printer, Abby, so I did that at home.'

He hauled a bundle of cables out, looked at the table and laughed. 'I'll put these back in the bag until I need them. This table is beginning to look like my desks at home.'

Surveying the now cluttered table, Harry pointed at the obviously much older laptop, heavy-looking and much thicker than the sleek modern one beside it. 'Is that your super secure laptop? Like an old one you kept on purpose?'

'Yep – there's stuff on it that I don't want near the internet. Like some of what I've saved for your use, for example. I used my third computer at home to do the sneaky stuff, the one with total breach protection and a very hard to track fingerprint, so to speak. I don't know how tech savvy you are, so I won't use tech speak, but let's say it's as safe as if it had a crocodile infested moat around it. So I did the tricky stuff from that machine, saved it on a USB stick and transferred it to this old banger and then I deleted every trace from the computer I'd used – the safest one. Just to make it nearly impossible for anyone to prove where all the bits of data I've planted in various places came from.'

Abby smiled at Harry's expression of awe and

curiosity. 'I told you he's worth his weight in gold, didn't I? And he's a very heavy guy, so his value is astronomical. I can't wait to find out all the details. Do we do this ID lesson before or after Astrid comes?'

Jasper though for few moments while Harry and Abigail waited silently. If anything about Harry's fake ID got out Jasper's career would be ruined, and he would face serious charges. The fact that Harry would become an object of media curiosity and investigation mattered less in comparison, as did the effect of Abigail's career. The decision about how much to tell Astrid had to be Jasper's.

Finally Jasper's focus returned. 'I think we'll keep these details to us three. I do trust Astrid, but she's impulsive, which is part of her charm, but it could lead to trouble. If she said something about Harry coming from another timestream or from 2029 she'd be able to recover the situation by pretending it was a silly joke, and nobody would believe her anyway. But this? No, I think not.'

'I asked her to come later in the afternoon without giving a reason. If she'd asked I would have used a shopping expedition or something as an excuse, so we could have some time together before she gets here, but your reason for not telling her is the same as mine, so it's all good. Let's do this right now.' Abigail gestured to the kitchen bench. 'We've got a pizza waiting to be put in the oven, so we can have lunch any time without any fuss.'

'OK,' said Jasper a few minutes later with both

his laptops open and Abigail and Harry sitting on either side of him. 'This is what I've set up and I've tested it, but I want you to see it, Harry, so you know it from visual experience, so to speak.'

Harry moved his chair to angle towards Jasper's and leaned forward. 'I can't wait!'

'I decided not to try to insert you into the Births, Deaths and Marriages database – too many potential snags. The more I thought about it, the riskier it seemed, so I did what we talked about before and made it so you're born in the UK, still with the name we agreed on, David Williams, but you're always called Harry. You don't have a middle name – you'll be harder to track as just plain David Williams. The birthdate is what we decided before, so that's what shows on your application for permanent residency in New Zealand, which you made in October 2016. I fudged a birth certificate to accompany the application, but you can't use it to get an NZ passport – it would be double-checked, and it doesn't exist in the UK records, it's just an image. On the residence application you stated that you were born in Bristol because it's a big city and if anyone asks for details of where you grew up you can say you moved a lot and attended half a dozen schools – anything to make the trail hard to follow.'

'Do you think they might try? And if so, why would they?' Abigail wondered if he'd thought of some potential lose end.

'No, there's no reason for anyone to suspect you're not who you say you are, provided you stay under the radar and don't get famous or commit a crime. Anyway, after applying for permanent resident status it was granted early in 2017. I couldn't make you a citizen here, too risky, and as I said, you can't apply for citizenship now, because that would require a current UK passport and/or birth certificate, neither of which we can produce, and there's nothing we can do about it. But you have enough history to fill in forms if you need to, and to hand out as general information. The fake permanent residency is real, so to speak, as is the certificate. It exists in the official records now and looks just like it would if they'd issued it in 2017. And you have a scanned image of the certificate to print out, like if they ask for when you apply for a driver's licence.'

He turned to Abigail and said plaintively. 'Abby, I'm starving. Can you bake that pizza and turn on the electric jug?'

'Oh God, I forgot the industrial strength tea! Sorry – coming right up. Just continue talking, I can listen while I do this. I put the pizza in the oven a few minutes ago.'

'Great! So where was I? Oh yes, you've never had an IRD number here and it's too risky to try to fudge one, and you can't apply for one now. Awkward questions would be asked, like why you haven't declared any income if you've spent so many years here - it's simply not worth the risk. You can always say you have private funds if anyone wonders what you live on. The best thing is for

Abigail to set up a company with her as the sole director to sell the mining info, because you can't even be a shareholder without an IRD tax number. You've never voted, so you're not on the electoral roll, though you can be if you like, the residency gives you the right. But I got you an NHI number.'

'A what?' asked Harry, who has sat mesmerised while Jasper showed him a screenshot of his fake residence permit and the British birth certificate and continued talking nearly non-stop. Abigail put his mug of tea beside him, still with the teabag and spoon in it the way he liked it.

'National Health Index number. A vital component of modern life.' Jasper tasted his tea, put the mug down and stirred it vigorously and took another sip, leaving the spoon and teabag in the mug. Harry looked at Abigal and grinned. 'He's clearly a genius and worth his weight in teabags, but the way he takes his tea - unbelievable!'

Jasper ignored the comment and picked up the thread again. 'You have no extensive record in the health system because you've been exceptionally healthy, never been admitted to hospital, never registered with a general practitioner, but you had a Covid vaccination in early 2021 and a booster in November that year, so you've got a bit of background. I added those last things when Abby told me you'd been vaccinated, so it looks like a track record. So now you can tell them your NHI number next time you go in. Just say Abby didn't know and forgot to ask you. Such an impulsive girl!'

'Great!' Abigail pushed some of the clutter to one side and put plates on the table. 'So now he's got a couple of vital bits of history, the permanent residency and a health system ID. That's all we need, I think. How hard was this?'

'The most difficult thing was the NHI number – I had to come up with some really stealthy moves to get that done, but once I managed to create the number the rest was fairly straight-forward. I think it's vital for you to have one in case you need surgery sometime in the future or have an accident. I had thought it would be hard to get the clean police record from the UK for your residency application to look right, but it wasn't.'

He turned to face Harry. 'I'm sorry I couldn't get you born in this country, mate – it would have been great, but it's too risky, so I thought with the permanent residency in place you're safe here. And when you hit sixty-five you'll be able to apply for the pension based on the residency data unless they change the rules. Or Abby will have to look after you. Where's that pizza, Abby? It smells ready to me.'

asper proved his versatility by eating pizza with one hand and occasionally taking a deep swallow of the beer Abigail put beside him while he continued both talking and handing out printed sheets for them to read.

'This is just so you can kind of see it in real life,' he explained. 'We'll bin most of these when we're finished. I'm leaving you with this little SSD drive and everything I've created is on it. The invented details you supposedly mentioned on your residency application twenty years ago including your police record from the UK - it's all on this drive. I don't think I mentioned that before, I think I got diverted with some other stuff – like hunger pains. You can print your residency permit from the drive, it's an exact copy of what they really looked like in 2017, or save the image to your laptop or phone, but the drive contains a permanent record of what I've done. And a few other things I'll tell you about in a minute. Oh, one of those pages has the invented details I used to bolster the residency application – you should memorise those in case you need to use them sometime.'

'Incredible!' said Harry. 'Thank you! I can't imagine how you managed to create all this for me. The stuff you can do it incredible – you could be a cybercriminal - I've just read about those. What did you call that little drive thing?'

Jasper picked it up and handed it to Harry. 'A solid state drive, an SSD, super effective way of storing stuff instead of your usual external hard drive or a USB stick. It isn't affected by magnetism, so the data is safe from being accidentally wiped, it's fully encrypted and passworded. It's also in a so-called military strength case, which you could probably run over with a tank, and it wouldn't crack. I've put an eight digit PIN on it, which you'll have to keep written down somewhere, but not in the same location as the drive, please. My professional reputation is closely linked to what's on that SSD.'

He pointed at the pad and pen beside Harry's laptop at the end of the table and Harry passed them to him. 'This is the PIN, write it somewhere so you don't forget. Not that I'm expecting you to need to use that drive now that you've seen the print-outs, but you might want to save the scan of your residence permit on your laptop or your phone. Just jot the PIN down somewhere. It's my birthdate, so not in any way related to this household.'

'I know when your birthday is – 11 January, but not the year,' said Abigail after a moment's thought.

'Six years before yours, so now you have the PIN in your head, good!'

They tidied up the table and Jasper put his belongings back in the satchel and held out the printouts he'd brought. 'Put these somewhere else now, and when you and Harry have read them properly, tear them up. I don't want Astrid to see them. So now to the last thing I want to show you. Let's look at it right away, it won't take long. I printed a copy for each of you, so you can make notes on it while we talk, but there's no need to tear these up, just keep them handy for reference. All this info is on the SSD too.'

Abigail sat down again and picked up one of the final two pages he put on the table and pushed the other in Harry's direction.

'Right!' Jasper was obviously pleased with himself. 'This is the fun part! I've located a very high-powered law firm in the US that specialises in mining concessions, or rights or whatever they're called. They seem to have a great reputation. They act for landowners, whole countries and regional authorities all over the place and orchestrate their dealings with major mining companies, make the initial approach, write very specialised contracts and monitor progress. They work on a percentage basis, like a commission, but I haven't been able to figure out what the percentage is. It's not mentioned on their website, but it's probably quite high. Based on what I've read about oil exploration I'm guessing around twenty percent, but it could be higher.'

He drank some more beer and sighed contentedly. 'The legal guys at this place all have specific interest areas they concentrate on, different types of mining like open cast or underground and different metals, one or two only deal with Asia for example. A couple of them seem to mainly handle the fallout down the track. Like slag heaps that collapse, environmental damage, ponds with toxic waste materials that leak, that kind of thing. It's all on the website, so you can identify the best one to approach yourself, Harry.'

'Excellent – I'd only just started thinking of how I would find someone to deal with this, or rather for Abigail to deal with, if we decide to go ahead with this. But as I said before, it's up to her. I can become a gardener or something to earn a living, as Astrid suggested. I don't need to be wealthy.'

'There's a bit more to it, though, read that last paragraph. I spent some time checking out options and it's clear that you don't want to sell the template as we called it or even mention it. You just offer to sell them the coordinates for that Brazilian site and say you think has gigantic potential and have the kind of contract that specifies how much they pay you once they've drilled core samples and confirmed that you're right. And then another step when they start mining, a kind of payment per yield, quite a complex calculation, but it seems that's how it's done. So first you get onto this legal outfit in the US, and make sure you don't tell them too much, then they get in touch with mining giants, and it goes from there, step by step.' He looked around as if he'd lost something and added, 'And also, when someone's bought the rights to the site, started mining and the whole thing's operational in a serious way, *then* you can offer to sell them you template for how to find more lithium – probably for another fortune.'

Just then the doorbell went, so Harry took both sheets of paper, folded them in half and put them on the keyboard of his laptop before he closed it. Abigail went to open the door and in seconds the atmosphere in the kitchen changed as if my magic and became a whirl of exclamations and laughter.

'Jasper, hi!' exclaimed Astrid smiling widely. 'What fun that you're here again! Hi, Harry, cool T-shirt! I hope you got vaccinated! Here's the dessert, I had to make a new one - I took the one I forgot to bring here to work, and we all ate it at morning tea!'

Astrid's exuberant chatter and her obvious curiosity about what had brought Jasper back for another visit created a noisy interval. Abigail busied herself making coffee and another mug of tea for Jasper, got out the three packets of biscuits Harry had impulse bought in the supermarket and waited patiently without taking part in the banter until the drinks were ready.

'Can someone please move that laptop?' She put the biscuit packets in the middle of the table. 'Here are your drinks. A new routine for you, Jasper. Yours has two teabags this time, so hopefully you don't need to leave the spoon in and risk poking you eye out. And Harry's choice of different biscuits instead of the selection I usually buy.'

37

*A*strid, who had no idea that Jasper hadn't just arrived, was happy to feel included in what was coming; her curiosity about what would be revealed next was nearly palpable. She's like a child with an unopened present, thought Abigail and watched her eyes moving from Harry to herself to Jasper, bright and expectant. She smiled to herself; the story about Katrina would be more than enough to keep Astrid's busy mind occupied instead of trying to find out the details of what Jasper had done to create a new identity for Harry.

'We have a new discovery to tell you about – something that's taken both of us a while to process. Possibly the most incredible coincidence either of us ever heard of.' Harry moved his head slowly from side to side as he contemplated how unbelievable it was, and Abigail nodded. Then his tone changed to very serious. 'But before we get to the real surprise I have a confession to make.'

Astrid's attention was now totally focused on Harry, and Jasper's hand stopped halfway to the plate of biscuits and settled back beside his mug. They listened to Harry telling them about his marriage, how he returned early from a trip to Wellington and overheard Katrina boasting to her friend about how she had conned him. Abigail watched Astrid's and Jasper's faces go through much the same sequence of emotions. First surprise, then shock, followed by pity and then surprise again, when he told them how he had left for Brazil without confronting Katrina after his friend told him about her lover.

'All I had was his name, I didn't know him at all. In fact, I'd never heard his name before my friend told me.' Harry gave them a wry smile. 'Barton Wilder was a surgeon at the hospital where Katrina worked. And before you ask, Abigail already asked the most relevant question. Why did Katrina take up with him after so successfully scamming me and getting access to my money, after all her planning and research? The only thing I can come up with is that she was either so full of lust and new love that she couldn't resist, or else her personality just impels her in the direction of anything new and shiny, so to speak. Something she needs to lay her hands on to satisfy some inner craving.'

Abigail met Harry's eyes and saw the message, 'Please take over now!' and spoke quickly before the dam holding back the questions and comments burst. 'But here is the real surprise.'

She handed Jasper and Astrid a print-out each of the two newspaper articles; the first one from 2021 with Mr Brooks' description of how the naked woman had appeared on his doorstep, and the second from the magazine article a year later. 'Read these first and then I'll tell you the rest.'

Jasper looked thoughtfully at the sheet of paper in his hand and then up at Harry. 'Don't tell me ...' but Abigail held up her hand, palm out, and said, 'No questions yet, just hold it for a few minutes longer.'

She described how they had decided what she say in the email, after they found out how to contact him. 'The last thing we wanted was for him to get alarmed on her behalf and refuse to talk to me,' she explained. 'We wanted as much information as we could get out of him about this woman – find out if he understood she had appeared from another timestream or not, because it was obvious he was protective of her, so we had to tread gently. We felt that the best way to get information out of him was by pretending I'd lost track of a friend in 2021, and not describing what she looked like, hoping he wouldn't ask. So it worked, he said I could call him, and we recorded the conversation. I'll play it for you now.'

Listening to the recording was nearly as shocking and revealing to Harry and Abigail as it was to the other two. Isn't it interesting, thought Abigail, as she watched the faces around the table, that hearing something recorded suddenly brings out new ideas. It's like you hear more in the tone of someone's voice than you did when you were actually talking to them.

When the recording ended, Jasper shook his head in disbelief. 'Bloody hell! I can't believe it – it's got to be her, doesn't it? But how the hell did it happen? Have you worked it out?'

And Astrid said slowly, 'That scar on her shoulder and arm! She *must* have been at the airport. But not to meet you, Harry, to go on a holiday with that Barton guy and her scar is just like yours. You're right, the coincidence is incredible!'

When Harry told them what he had already told Abigail, that there had only been one airport for international flights in his timestream, and that Katrina hadn't known when he was coming back from Brazil, a stream of questions and comments followed.

'So you can see how it happened,' he said when the questions finally ended. 'But the fact that it happened at all is truly incredible, hard to believe.'

'Cosmic coincidence! In the true meaning of the word,' exclaimed Astid and they all smiled at her. She's a very lucky girl now, having these great guys in her life, thought Abigail, and that's another cosmic coincidence.

'I don't suppose you'll contact her?' Jasper looked searchingly at Harry. 'There wouldn't be any point, would it? I mean, you're not married to her here and now, and you don't want to be. Just ignoring it seems like the best idea. Are you going to try to find other victims from that ball lightning incident?'

'God, no! I'm happy to just be here, there's no point in trying even. What are the chances that someone else ended up here and remembered their past, like I did? I don't know why I tried in the first place - it seems stupid now. It could have exposed me to risk, made a normal life impossible. But we thought you two would enjoy hearing about this crazy coincidence.'

'Harry might be an anomaly,' said Abigail thoughtfully. 'There might be more of them, but it's possible he's the only one who arrived with his whole memory intact, but we'll never know, and it doesn't matter, does it? Only we four know about him and that's how it will stay - forever.'

After dinner, with Astrid's apple and cinnamon cake in front of them Astrid asked to hear the recording again. 'Recording it was a *great* idea! And though she was evil and scammed you, Harry, I think it's nice that she's being looked after by Mr Brooks – and that she's got her gardener boyfriend. She might have ended up kind of mentally destroyed otherwise.'

'So now we get to the other arm of this strange coincidence.' Abigail had never been able to quite let go of theorising about the timestream concept. 'When Harry materialised on my front lawn, we speculated about why he got shifted to 2026, and then we decided it might be that his timestream and ours are three years out of step, and he got moved straight sideways, so to speak. But as Harry's pointed out, perhaps there are more dimensions and a different logic that we don't even know about and finding that Katrina was moved from 2029 to 2021 and has now been here for five years - that was a surprise. It blew all our theories out of the water.'

Jasper smiled and raised his glass in a mock toast. 'As somebody famously said recently, it doesn't matter, does it? We'll never know.'

EPILOGUE

ONE YEAR LATER

Abigail drove into the garage, took the shopping off the back seat and went through to the kitchen where the scene that met her eyes was the same as nearly every other day when she came home in the early afternoon from her now part-time job at the Court. Already a little routine had developed, and she had only been back a few weeks. Harry was at the kitchen table with a book and a mug of coffee in front of him. Six baby bottles full of formula were cooling on the bench ready to go into the fridge, and two baby pods were suspended side by side, gently swinging from hooks in the ceiling.

'Oh look at them!' Abigail dropped her shopping bags on the bench and went over to look down at the twins, who were sound asleep, the way only babies can sleep, as if utterly lost in time. 'Just so content with the movement. Have they been good?'

Harry laughed. 'Of course - they're always good.

I'm hoping we won't have any drama until they're teenagers. I think we did a really good job creating those two.' He reached out and pushed first one and then the other pod and set them swinging again. 'And Rosie is now far better at burping than Jasper. You would have thought that having Jasper senior for a godfather would have turned him into a burping male, but no - he still needs a hand patting his back.'

Suddenly Abigail remembered and shook her head at herself. 'God! I'm sorry, I forgot. I was going to forward an email I got this morning and then I got busy and forgot. Carl Rodman sent a long update and said he got a bite from that second mining corporation he wrote about a couple of weeks ago. He said he feels good about it, and they've accepted the back story, no questions at all – probably because he himself believes it. He's about to start negotiating, but before he does that, he wants to know if we want to change any of the instructions we originally gave him. Should I ask him to change anything? Have you thought about anything else you want to add?'

'No, let it stand as it is. I think I spent enough time getting it right before we engaged him.'

It was unbelievable, thought Abigail, as she unpacked the groceries and sat down with a cup of coffee. The unexpected things that had fallen into place in the last six or seven months without a hitch, not what she had expected at all. After having to take four months of parental leave before the twins were born when her blood pressure suddenly shot up, she had expected her application to split her position, so she could work part time to be refused, but it had been approved. And discovering what a great stay-at-home dad Harry had turned into was another.

'Born to be a dad.' Astrid had said a couple days ago. 'Best one ever! I'll share him with the twins.'

Jasper had suggested that they told anyone who wondered what Harry did for a living, that he worked online as a consultant.

'And let's face it,' Abigail had said soon after the twins were born. 'I can't find it in myself to have people think I'm just living off insurance money or your income, darling. I need to at least have a part time job.'

Nobody had questioned it since they first mentioned it to a few of their friends, and even Rosemary, who had often in the past been best at picking up on evasive comments, had accepted it with no questions asked.

The last thing now, not counting the possible mining rights contract, was to buy Astrid an apartment and gift it to her. With everything that had been going on they just hadn't got around to it, but now they must and Harry's idea to gently moderate the effect of Astrid having one major expense removed would be part of the deal. She would have to promise him – the one person she would always keep a promise to – that she would put a certain amount into a savings account every payday.

'It will amount to quite a bit over a few years instead of being spent on things she probably doesn't need,' he had said to Abigail when he launched the idea. 'And eventually she'll ask if she can spend it on buying a house or an electric car, and we'll say yes.'

'Do you think we're luckier than we deserve, or at least I am? Things have turned out so unexpectedly well for us that I feel guilty sometimes,' she said that night over bowls of ice cream with Baileys, and Harry looked up from his book and waited without comment, the way he often did when he sensed there was more to come. 'You deserve to reap the benefits of what you discovered through your own clever work, but I was handed things on a plate – including you in a way. I want to share my luck a bit wider than just buying an apartment for Astrid.'

She gestured with her spoon, watched Harry's eyes track it as he always did and grinned. 'It's been *very* properly licked! But seriously, I want to do something for others with all that money Mike organised for me, use it to improve things for people who can't do it for themselves, but who deserve a chance of something better. Not like general welfare but maybe if we hear about a person who's had some rotten luck and might never get back on track – that kind of person.'

'Did you read my notes, or did you just read my mind again?' Harry smiled and shook his head. 'Last week I wrote myself a little list of worthwhile things we can do if that mining deal comes off. Very much on the lines of what you've just said. I've been given a second chance by being shunted sideways from a dystopian timestream to this one, so why not share it, as you say. There's nothing to stop us, is there?'

'I didn't read your notes, but we often think the same – another lucky thing.'

'You know what the biggest piece of luck is? That you were living in this house in this timestream. Or none of this would have happened.' Harry's eyes were serious. 'I often think about what a miserable and confused life I might have had if you hadn't been here to open the door that night.'

There was no need to say anything more; they just smiled at each other and went back to reading.

THANK YOU

We hope you've enjoyed reading this story and would consider leaving a review, or even a rating.

These are not only much appreciated, they also help other readers discover new authors.

For other titles from Lightpool Publishing, please read on.

ABOUT SASKIA

Saskia Woodhill is an author of soft romance novels where slightly paranormal characters occasionally engage in outrageous behaviour and sometimes find themselves in funny or dangerous situations - or funny and dangerous at the same time. Stories that will make you laugh and cry and turn the pages to a satisfying ending.

ALSO FROM SASKIA

Alba's abrupt exit in the middle of an interview for a dream job sets off a chain of events she never saw coming. The inexplicable dread she occasionally feels isn't her imagination, it's a warning signal, one that others don't sense. But this time simply walking away wasn't enough - now a powerful man is determined to discover why she left.

Follow Alba on her intense, emotional journey of secrets, risk-taking and life-changing decisions into a world where the stakes are high, trust is precious, and her future hangs in the balance. This story will keep you riveted, questioning fate and the power of love.

Available from all good bookshops.

Julia, owner of a successful garage and used to working with men, prides herself on her practical and down-to-earth nature. But her calm and orderly world is about to change forever.

After a concussion, she disturbingly starts hearing the thoughts of others as spoken words in her mind. First, it's her sister, then it's Milton, the sexy customer with the sarcastic smile, and the man Julia is irresistibly drawn to, despite his outrageous thoughts.

Available from all good bookshops

OTHER TITLES FROM
LIGHTPOOL PUBLISHING

Letters from the Past by Tina Clough is a series of stand-alone novels where a letter from or about the past reveals something that changes a woman's perceptions of her family, and affects her outlook on life. Life can change in a moment and sometimes you have to step into the unknown and take a chance on love.

Having had nobody in her life since her husband died, Lara unexpectedly finds herself involved with three men. One is planning to use her, one she plans to use for her own ends, and one becomes a "friend-with-benefits" with surprising results. Sometimes a quiet schoolteacher is not all she seems at first glance.

Callista experiences an event of apparent ESP at the Okehampton Castle ruins and becomes a media sensation, but the effect it has on her life is dramatic. How do two people, one calm. one seriously claustrophobic, who feel they are poles apart, cope for an hour and a half in total darkness in a stalled lift? And can they handle the consequences?

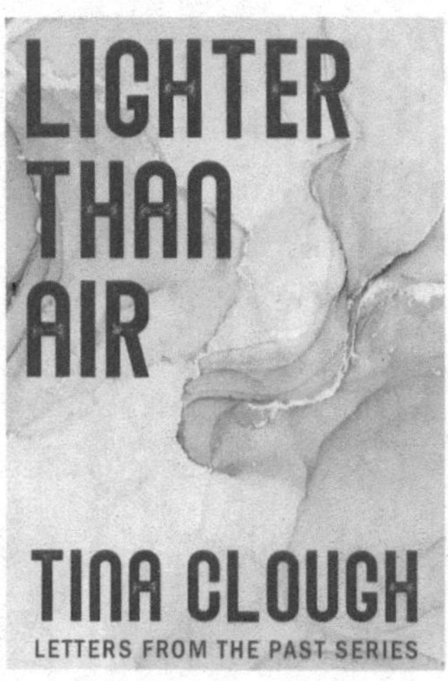

Sofia's life is in turmoil: a difficult diva mother, a letter with a confession about a family killing and having to accept help from a man she loathes when she is injured. Can reluctant attraction turn into love?

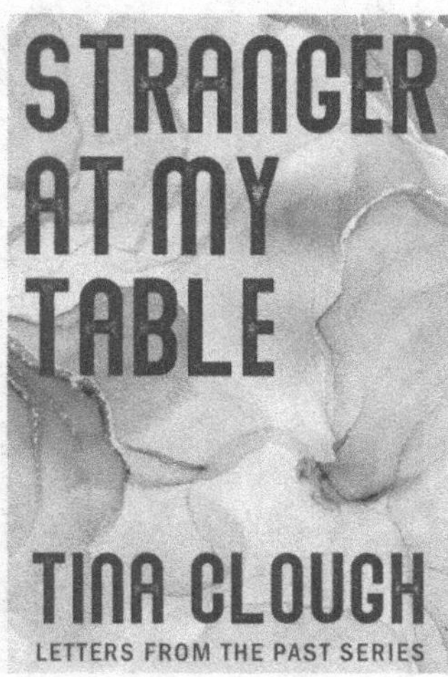

Who is the stranger living in the empty house Miranda inherited from her grandmother? Why is he living like a secretive recluse in someone else's house? Reckless Miranda decides to confront him, and what she discovers prompts her to set out on a fearless quest to bring justice to a man who has given up hope. But is the gamble too great or a risk worth taking?

When Emma finds an old letter in a library book she is instantly intrigued, but by researching the origin of the letter she unwittingly opens the door to danger and becomes the target for threats and harassment. Nearly desperate, she takes a leap of blind faith into the unknown and accepts an offer of help from a stranger - but can she trust him?

Jamie, an ardent protester against the gigantic Vista Resort development and Leo Masters, the high-powered developer, seem unlikely to ever agree on anything. But unexpected coincidences and chance brings them together in a fragile state of mutual respect. Will courage and kindness resolve the situation, or do they need help?

After a bizarre accident with ESP overtones, the media haunt Arapera. But can she trust an offer of help from a man she has only met once? Or will she regret it for the rest of her life if she doesn't take the chance? Sometimes life is a knife-edge balance between staying safe and taking risks, and there is no way of predicting if the gamble is worth it.

When crime-writer Saskia finds an unconscious stranger, she has a strange and strong emotional connection. Pretending to be his cousin and with no thought for the consequences, she spends weeks at his hospital bedside. But what will happen when he wakes and discovers she has invaded his life, breached his privacy and made crucial decisions on his behalf?

THE GIRL WHO LIVED TWICE

What would you do if you woke up one morning and found that time had rewound exactly a year? Would you revisit your past mistakes and try to do better? Would you try to get revenge on those who had wronged you? Or would you use what you knew to get rich? When Mia finds herself in her own past, she must decide how best to use her pre-knowledge of one year's worth of events and personal issues.